**This book is to be returned on or before
the last date stamped below.**

Annie's Kingdom

Annie's Kingdom

Sarah Shears

PIATKUS

© Sarah Shears 1980

First published in Great Britain by
Judy Piatkus (Publishers) Limited of Loughton, Essex

British Library Cataloguing in Publication Data

Shears, Sarah
   Annie's Kingdom.
   Vol. 3
   I. Title
   823′ .9′1F   PR6069.H3955A/
   ISBN 0–86188–056–0

Photoset, printed and bound in Great Britain by
REDWOOD BURN LIMITED
Trowbridge & Esher

Chapter One

When Annie Parsons' eldest son, Stan, was discharged from the Army in the Spring of 1919, he came back to his cottage home in the Kent village to pick up the threads of his livelihood in the garden workshop.

He sadly missed his girl-wife, Kathie, who had sat for hours on a kitchen chair in the workshop nursing a cat on her lap. But Kathie's name was never mentioned now. She had died in childbirth – and Stan was not the father of the child, but his youngest brother, Gordon.

It was inconceivable to Annie that such blatant treachery should actually have happened in her own family, and that her first-born had threatened to murder her youngest if he ever set foot in the house again.

Annie had always loved her four boys more devotedly than her husband, Teddy, for maternity was strong in her quiet nature. Persuaded into marriage with the feckless Teddy at the age of seventeen, Annie had brought up her four boys almost single-handed in proud poverty.

For Teddy and Annie at the age of thirteen from their respective institutions there had been no alternative but 'service'. The strict hierarchy of the servants' hall had been as impossible to penetrate as the titled family they served. For Annie, the third housemaid, and Teddy, the 'boots boy' the abundant food fully compensated for the long hours of drudgery. Annie would have been content to spent the rest of her life at Merton Hall for she was born to serve, and was constantly reminded of the hymn all the orphaned

1

children had learned by heart:-

> *The rich man in his castle*
> *The poor man at his gate,*
> *God made them high or lowly,*
> *And ordered their estate.*

Not so, Teddy, who saw himself moving into a more affluent society, and declared it was just the luck of the draw whether you were born in a mansion or a hovel.

Marriage was no substitute for freedom. Teddy was like a wild bird in a cage, so Annie opened the door and set him free to go his own way. Stan, Dick, Tom and Gordon were as different as any four boys could possibly be, but as 'Gran' (her old neighbour) pointed out so sensibly when Tom arrived on the scene with red hair, 'You 'as to expect a few surprises, my girl, when you an' Teddy is both orphans'.

It was true, of course. Where, for instance, did Stan get his taste for mechanics, or Dick his clever brain? Tom's red head was the match for Annie's dark head or Teddy's fairness.

As for Gordon, who asked nothing more than to be left alone with a paint-box and brush, he was the least understood of all Annie's boys. An artist in the family was almost an embarrassment!

After a few weeks had passed, it seemed Stan had never been away, and Annie found the tapping and hammering a musical accompaniment to her chores. The bicycles were leaning on the outside wall of the house, awaiting repairs, and the smell of oil permeated his clothes.

Annie's firstborn had always been inarticulate, but once they had been close in understanding, for Stan was a kind and thoughtful person. The silent meals were no longer companionable, but strained, and they did not linger at the table when the food was eaten, but went their separate ways. However, they shared a common bond in work, for mother and son could not sit idle. All day he was busy in his workshop, for customers brought their old machines to be serviced, and many were sadly in need of new tyres and brakes. Few could afford the costly new models coming on to the market, and Stan was obliged to patch up the old. Most of these machines had been used by the children when the men in the family went away to war – and few came back to claim them. The men had taken pride in their machines, oiling and cleaning them regularly, and some had bought puncture outfits from Stan and preferred to mend their own punctures. They were mostly trades-people and the lower middle-class who had owned bicycles before the war, for working-class men used Shanks's pony and daughters in service would walk long distances to visit their parents on their free Sunday afternoons.

The boys and girls had missed the strict discipline nor-mally imposed by fathers and elder brothers before the war, and were running wild without supervision. Over-worked mothers worried by rationing, and the problem of feeding their large families, suffering the loss of their menfolk on the Western Front, had loosened the tight reins of parental authority, and their offspring were taking liberties undreamed of before the war. Fighting and pushing, they crowded into Stan's workshop, demanding immediate attention, but Stan ordered them outside and made them take their turn. In his quiet way he managed to convey his dislike of such unruly behaviour. He soon recognised the need of some kind of club for the boys, and he got permission to re-form the company of Boy Scouts in the village.

A strong contingent of some forty girls between the ages of ten and fourteen had been operating during the war since the ladies of the gentry had given their services and lent their gardens to the Girl Guides. The boys had envied their lucky sisters in their smart blue uniforms, for all children

3

love a uniform, and now they could hardly wait to join the ranks of the newly-enrolled Scouts.

They met one evening a week in the crowded Army hut, and on Saturday afternoons they assembled outside Annie's cottage and marched away in cheerful song to their outdoor activities in the fields and woods. It was not only harassed mothers who blessed Stan for giving up his time to the boys, but Annie was delighted to see him absorbed in this new interest. The bitterness that had soured his young life of recent years was forgotten, and the boys liked and respected their Scoutmaster. He encouraged them to work for the money they needed to buy their uniforms, and gave them a sense of pride in the jobs they found to do after school and Saturday mornings. Competition was keen, and Stan was amazed at their initiative, for he and his brothers had been somewhat conservative in their schooldays, deciding either to deliver papers or help the milkman on his round. Now two of Stan's boys were busy with buckets and shovels at the blacksmith's forge, and selling the dung to regular customers as a fertiliser for their gardens. Several boys were kept busy every Saturday morning cleaning windows and knives for elderly spinster ladies whose servants had deserted them.

There were gardens to be dug, hedges to be trimmed, wood to chop, stables to be cleaned out and horses to groom. One enterprising lad with the makings of a business tycoon collected rags, newspapers and scrap iron on a hand cart and sold them to a dealer. There was a big rush to join the ranks by the few reluctant lads who had not been so keen on the work and discipline involved in this 'Boy Scout lark' when it was announced there would be a summer camp. They stormed Stan's workshop in their eagerness to join!

The first fortnight in August had been decided on, before the start of the six-week hop-picking when all the

4

village children were expected to help, until they left school. Mothers were persuaded to lend dark blankets and a jumble sale was organised in the village hall to raise funds for tents and camping equipment.

'That Stan Parsons has found his true vocation at last,' they said of him.

In his neat khaki tunic, shorts and hat, with highly polished shoes, he was hardly recognisable. The greasy overalls were discarded, grimed hands scrubbed, and ruffled hair smoothed. The transformation was not only pleasing to Annie, but a shining example to the boys.

'Will Stan forgive his brother Gordon now?' Annie asked herself in that post-war year of readjustment. Would his new responsibilities and the vows he had taken with such earnestness remind him to be generous in forgiveness to his own brother, his own brother who had seduced his wife? Time would prove whether the splendid purposes and principles of the Scout movement would be stronger than his own stubborn prejudices.

There was so much heartache for Annie with her blinded son Tom still living at the hostel in London and Dick in Somerset. Gordon had disappeared. Her boys were scattered. The war was to blame for the shattering of all Annie's bright hopes for the future. She had anticipated their marriage to local girls and her own pride and joy in being a grandmother.

'You're lucky, Mrs Parsons, with all your boys still living. Some mothers lost two or three sons,' she was reminded in the village. It was true and she was shamed by her selfishness and thereafter kept a still tongue in her head.

Stan had told her he would never marry again, and he hardly noticed the emancipated young women, no longer slaves to domestic service, but working as shop assistants, clerks and typists, machine operators in factories, porters and postmen.

It was Stan who travelled to London now every third Sunday to visit Tom, but he found his younger brother sadly changed, and the visits distressing and disappointing. The compassionate tears that welled in his eyes were lost on Tom, who could not see them, and the firm grip of Stan's hand was too quickly over for lasting reassurance. It was impossible for Stan to realise the anguish and frustration of that darkened world – impossible for Tom to describe it, or to explain the importance of touch to a blinded person.

In these early months of rehabilitation he was only at ease with the fellows and the teachers at the hostel, and any outside visitor, even his own brother, was regarded with suspicion. He did not want pity from anyone, and Stan was met with the same stubborn resistance to kindness and sympathy as his mother found on her first and only visit to London.

'I shall bloody well manage to earn a living, somehow. I'm not daft and I'm not deaf, though some folks seem to think so. Don't you worry. I don't intend to sit around like a bloody parasite!' he told Stan.

The jutting chin, the grim mouth and the swearing all conveyed a fierce determination for independence, but what did the future hold for Tom when he left the shelter of the hostel and the companions who shared his grievous misfortune?

'It's marvellous what he can manage to do for himself after only six months,' Stan told his mother. 'Tom has always been so strong and healthy, hasn't he? They tell me he walks for miles round and round the enclosed garden on the handrail for he's so restless and frustrated. So much of the day is spent indoors on tedious tasks, but it's all part of the training, so Tom must conform or get out. I watched

6

the class at work on basket-making and another class learning to weave on handlooms. Tom was sitting by an open window with his face lifted, and his hands were plaiting raffia rather slowly and clumsily. We can't let him spend the rest of his days making baskets. He would go crazy, but what can we do with him? I couldn't bear to watch him, so I went outside and waited till the class was dismissed and he was free to talk to me. I felt I was intruding, that he would resent me staring at him in an unguarded moment. Oh, Mum! What are we going to do with him when he comes home? He can't stay at the hostel after he has finished the training period for there's a long waiting list. I made enquiries after I left Tom, and I was told he would be coming home for a holiday, and would be helped to find a place in a workshop for the blind, but it would not be easy unless he was prepared to live in London. Alternatively, he could be provided with equipment and materials to work at home, but would have to find a market for his work. What do you think? I could build him a little workshop next to mine, and we could take long walks together. I wonder?'

Stan sighed with the weight of the burden he had taken on his own shoulders while Annie wept quietly for the boy she had lost – the boy who once had leapt over gates and fences, climbed the highest trees and dared his brothers to dangerous pranks. Tom was born to lead, not to be led. His whole mentality was different from his brothers. Even in the cradle he had asserted himself with roars of rage and flung his toys on the floor. 'Poor Tom – oh, my poor boy,' moaned Annie. 'What are we going to do with him?'

Stan put a comforting arm about her shoulders. She leaned on him now. The war had aged all the mothers in the village and the only joy was in the birth of a child. Life went on. A new generation of boys would grow up to replace the sons who had died.

For Annie there was only Dick to father a child and there

7

was no mention of his wife in his last letter. Dick had married the daughter of Doctor Pearce by special licence in the Convalescent Home in Somerset. She was a nursing sister in the Field Hospital where Dick had almost died from the aftermath of gas poisoning. She was not yet free to settle down to civilian life, or to raise a family, and Annie had doubts about the marriage. It was not considered a suitable match and Annie was so class conscious she felt embarrassed when she encountered Dr Pearce.

It was Tom who would need all her love and attention when he came home, and Stan's suggestion about the workshop was a good one.

'Shall you mention it when you see him again?' she asked him.

'Yes. It will give him something to think about, and if he likes the idea I can start on it.'

Annie dried her eyes. 'You're a good boy, Stan. Whatever should I do without you,' she said gratefully.

Tom came home in the spring of 1920. Half-reluctant to leave the hostel and its familiar ways, familiar smells and sounds, familiar voices, and the good fellowship of his blinded companions, he was nervous and irritable.

From the moment that he stepped out of the train on to the platform, and stood, with lifted, listening face to hear his brother's running footsteps, Tom was alone and isolated in his dark little world that neither his brother nor his mother could penetrate.

They climbed the hill together, arm in arm, Stan carrying the heavy kitbag slung over his shoulder. Birds twittered in the hedges, children ran past shouting with excitement. The long hard winter was over. Primroses clustered on the steep banks of the ditches, lambs gambolled on their spindly legs, daffodils lifted golden heads in the lush green grass of Farmer Clarke's meadow, and the warm scent of wallflowers was sweet in cottage gardens; but only Stan was aware of the miracle of spring, and only Stan could see the scudding clouds, the rooks nesting in the tall elms, and the man following the plough in a distant field.

Not till this hour of this particular day when the brothers climbed the hill together was Stan fully aware of Tom's deprivation. Surrounded by companions, walking confidently about the house and garden by the guiding rails, Tom had reached a stage of independence that surprised and delighted the dedicated members of the staff. Now, in this strange environment he could not recognise or even associate it with his boyhood; he was confused and frightened and clung like a lost child to Stan's arm. He did not want to hear about the workshop that Stan had erected, or the materials that had already been delivered, or the promise of a regular customer for his baskets.

'The postmistress will take all your work, Tom, to sell in the shop. She said she would hang the baskets on hooks in the ceiling to attract the customers who came to do business at the post-office counter. She's a wonderful woman, the postmistress, always ready to help a good cause.'

Stan's voice trailed away for there was no response in his brother's blank face. He had worked so hard on the hut that adjoined his own, and neglected his own customers in his eagerness to have everything ready for Tom's homecoming. The Scouts had helped on Saturday afternoons, giving up their normal outdoor activities and swarming like bees round a honeypot. Annie had provided jugs of lemonade and currant buns. All the boys knew about Tom Parsons, and were curious to meet their leader's brother who could not see where he was going.

'We'll take him along with us when we go camping, won't we, sir?' said one.

'We'll look after him, Sir, don't you worry,' said another.

9

That 'sir' was still a little embarrassing to Stan's unpretentious personality, but a source of much pride to Annie, who had not expected Stan to be so respected. He was not a born leader and his shyness and diffidence had to be conquered before he had acquired that confident assurance the boys required.

Now Stan was wondering whether his noisy, exuberant boys would upset Tom, and if their good intentions were received with this same blank expression they would soon be discouraged. This homecoming for which he had worked and planned for so long was already dampened by Tom's total lack of interest.

'So, I'm another good cause, am I?' he demanded. 'Oh well, it's a change from the Waifs and Strays and the Missions to Seamen. Perhaps the postmistress will have a collecting box on the counter?' The bitterness in his voice brought the tears flooding his brother's sighted eyes, and Stan had no answer, no weapons with which to defend himself against this young stranger who clutched his arm. Would the tension between them upset the happy, relaxed atmosphere that he and his mother had been enjoying for some time?

'Hello, Stan!' a cheery voice called from the doorway of the grocer's shop as they started up the High Street. Then, as an afterthought, 'Hello, Tom!'

Stan lifted a hand in salute and his nervous smile was not lost on the grocer. Tom turned his head and muttered, 'hello' like an obedient child who has been trained to answer.

'It's a cruel shame. Tom was always the liveliest of Annie Parsons' boys,' the grocer reflected. 'That poor woman has taken some hard knocks in her time, but I reckon this is the hardest.'

Three months had passed and Tom had settled down to his

tedious work routine with grim determination. The door of his little workshop was never closed, so Annie could watch him at work from her scullery window. Yet, in this anxious watching she was conscious of taking an unfair advantage of Tom's blindness. She was saddened by her failure to make contact with this boy whose need of love and understanding was more urgent than ever before in his young life. His pride and independence had become a barrier and he scorned the many offers of help so abruptly that well-meaning sympathisers soon drifted away.

'I don't want pity from anyone,' he reminded his mother and brother repeatedly in those early weeks of re-adjustment, and they would glance at each other and shake their heads over his obstinacy. Although he rejected human contact, he accepted the canine quite naturally, since Tom had always been fond of dogs.

Ben, the Welsh collie, lay at his feet, his head resting on Tom's boots, while the busy fingers plaited and weaved with clumsy impatience. The few shillings that he earned from the sale of his baskets did not compensate Annie for all the extra food she had to provide, for Tom was a hearty eater and meals were regarded as a welcome diversion in the long hours he spent in his workshop.

Stan would buy his brother tobacco for a pipe he liked to smoke after supper, as it seemed to soothe the nervous tensions of the busy day.

When Tom sighed with boredom, Ben would plant his paws on his lap and gaze up at his master with limpid adoring eyes. The affinity between them was touching, and only Ben could coax a smile to that blank face, or a tender word from the silent tongue.

'Good fellow. Good old Ben. You understand, don't you boy? You and me can manage without the rest,' Annie overheard one evening – and her heart ached with pity and love. This awareness of watching and listening for his every movement was not lost on Tom, and he found it increasingly irksome. He was smothered in their kindness. He had to get away – but how? – where?

One evening, when Stan had explained he must finish an urgent job, and they would take a walk later, Tom's patience was exhausted. He tied a handkerchief round Ben's neck, slipped through a plaited strand of raffia, and whispered hoarsely, 'Walk, Ben.'

The dog always accompanied them on their walks, racing ahead, barking excitedly as glad to be released from the workshop as his young master. Now he stood, hesitating, wagging his tail, uncertain what was expected of him.

'Walk, Ben,' Tom repeated, more urgently. He could hear the hum of a sewing machine in the adjoining hut, and his mother would be busy with her interminable knitting in the front porch, where she liked to spend the last hour of the day before bedtime.

Cautiously, the dog moved forward and Tom followed, clutching the leash, every sense alert to the shared danger. He could feel the slight rise of the garden path and the hens cackled noisily as the dog passed. When Ben pulled up suddenly at the fence, Tom cracked his head on an overhanging branch and swore testily. Momentarily surprised by the impact, his heart thumped, and he stood quite still to summon the courage to take another step into this hostile world that awaited him beyond the safety of the workshop. He had climbed over this fence a score of times with Stan of recent weeks, he reasoned sensibly, so why not follow Ben, whose canine intelligence was surely equal to any human? He could feel the bruise swelling on his forehead, but it was not the first time he had collided with a hard obstacle and it wouldn't be the last.

'Over, Ben!' he ordered.

The dog scrambled over easily and Tom followed, one hand reaching out for guidance. From now on it would be

12

instinctive, this groping hand reaching out to the unseen obstacles in his path. Now he could feel the grass under his feet, and they stood there for a long moment while he filled his lungs with the cool, sweet breath of a summer evening, all his pulses leaping with excitement of his own daring. Why, he knew every inch of this field! The sheep should be grazing in this field, but they would soon scatter when they saw Ben. Some distance away – it was difficult now to judge distances – was a circle of fir trees. Once upon a time he could climb those trees like a monkey. He grinned at the memory of his recklessness. Swaying perilously on a topmost branch, he would wave to Dick and Gordon who did not climb trees. He remembered how small they looked, standing together in the field, their uplifted faces white and scared. Stan would be yelling at him from a lower branch, 'Come down! Do you hear me, Tom? Come down, you little fool!' But he laughed and waved and felt like a king sitting on the top of the highest tree.

He felt like a king now, surprisingly. It was a different kind of achievement, but still it *was* an adventure for a fellow who couldn't see where he was going!

He bent down to pat Ben's head. 'Walk, boy!'

The dog responded instantly now, and there was no more hesitation as they went forward, the dog leading, the man following, one hand gripping the leash, the other outstretched.

'Mum! Mum! Come quickly! Tom's gone!'

Stan's urgent cry of alarm brought Annie hurrying to the door, and they ran together down the garden path.

'He can't have gone far, he was here half an hour ago,' Stan panted.

When they reached the fence they stopped dead and gazed in astonishment at the retreating back of Tom and the dog. They could see Tom's red head lifted proudly, but

Stan was frowning.

'Why couldn't he wait? I told him I had an urgent job to finish. He's so darn impatient,' he sighed. It had been a long hot day in his own workshop. 'It's too risky, Mum. He could have a nasty accident' – and his mother agreed.

Tom was so self-willed, so difficult to live with these days. He wanted his own way all the time, no matter the trouble and inconvenience to others. They were both a little afraid of this glowering stranger with the sightless eyes. Neither could see the courage or the purpose of such a foolhardy escapade, only the danger. And because their devotion was too over-cautious, they would never know the pleasure the dog was already enjoying with Tom. They saw the sturdy figure trip and stumble. They saw him fall. They saw him sprawled on the rough grass, his arms spreadeagled, his face buried.

Annie covered her mouth to hold back the scream and climbed on the fence, but Stan held her back.

'Leave him, Mum. Leave him, for God's sake.'

Tom lay still, the dog pawing at his hidden face. It was a moment of poignant suspense they would always remember. Was he hurt? Was he crying?

Then, as suddenly as he had fallen, he rolled over on his back, opened his arms, and the dog leapt on his chest, barking excitedly, licking his face.

'He's laughing, Mum – *Tom's laughing*,' said Stan, in a choked voice.

It was true. That merry, rollicking laugh they had thought never to hear again was spilling out of him, mingled with the sharp yapping of the dog. Stan put his arm about his mother's shoulders and they turned away, to walk slowly back down the garden path. They seemed to know that a crisis had been reached, but they could not begin to understand what it meant to Tom – the thrill and the satisfaction in that first independent walk.

14

'I'm coming with you, Mum,' said Tom decidedly.

It was the first morning of the hop-picking season, and Annie had been up since five to leave everything ready for Stan, who said he could manage to cope. They needed those few extra pounds she could earn in the hop-gardens more than ever this year, and she was looking forward to the six weeks when she would escape from the house and the constant strain of living with a severely handicapped person.

She was spreading butter on several slices of home-baked bread and two slices of bacon would make the few sandwiches she required for her own dinner. With a thick chunk of bread pudding she had baked the previous day and a flask of tea, she would satisfy the healthy appetite she always enjoyed in the hop-garden.

In those early years in service at Merton Hall, Annie had been fed so well she put on weight, and in four years was 'as plump as a spring chicken' according to Cook. Even in the years of privation when she often went without a meal when her growing boys demanded something to eat at all hours of the day, Annie still kept her plump little figure. In those days she ate what was left over, or served herself the smallest portion of meat with a lot of vegetables. Children do not notice what their mothers are eating. They are much too concerned with their own share! Dick and Gordon had always been finicky eaters, and now Tom was finicky and often critical of the food he found on his plate. Thank God for Stan, Annie would remind herself when her patience was wearing thin. Now she looked up in surprise to see Tom standing in the doorway of the staircase, for it was barely six o'clock and he usually slept late. The dog was close at his heels for he slept on Tom's bed. They were inseparable companions, day and night. Annie had raised no objection to this arrangement though she had always main-

15

tained a firm ruling – one of the few rules the boys had to respect – 'no animals upstairs'.

Tom's face was red and shining from its morning scrub, his hair plastered with water. He was wearing the old cord-uroy breeches and plaid shirt he had once worn on the farm, and the heavy gum-boots. The collar of the shirt was turned down and the buttons unfastened, and Annie could see the thick hairs on his chest and the strong muscles in his arms over the rolled sleeves. He scorned a vest, as he scorned a jacket or an overcoat in winter. He looked very sturdy and manly standing there, with his thrusting chin and bold manner.

'Coming – with – me?' Annie echoed, stupidly, all her hopes dwindling in the baleful stare of those sightless eyes.

'Why not? I'm fed up with staying indoors. Besides, I want to see the old haunts again.' He always spoke this way – of seeing things he would never see again, and Annie found it strange and rather uncanny.

She sighed with a sense of being trapped, and Tom must have known he was being awkward. For some years his mother had enjoyed this season of hop-picking on her own, but even when they were children, she had regarded it as a nice change and not as a hard, laborious task to be endured for the sake of those few extra pounds.

'Well, in that case I must pack some extra food,' she said, briskly. 'You can have the sausage rolls you were going to have for your dinner anyway, and I'll make a few cheese sandwiches.'

'Don't forget the pickle,' Tom reminded her.

'Would you like a slice of cake or gingerbread for your elevenses – or both?'

'Both,' said Tom, stepping down into the living-room to supervise the menu. He could hear the fire crackling and the canary chirping. He could smell the bacon but he did not care for it because it was too fat. They could only afford

16

the cheapest cut.

'How about fruit? – a pear or an apple?' Annie was bustling about collecting provisions.

'Both,' Tom repeated, and Annie laughed nervously. What would she do with Tom in the hop-garden? How could he pick hops he could not see? He would have Ben, of course, so perhaps they would wander away together for at least part of the day and leave her alone. Now she was being selfish and she must check this longing to get away from Tom and his bullying manner. 'I want – I will – Do this – Do that.' He never said 'please' or 'thank you.'

'I've only the one flask, Tom,' she reminded him, tentatively.

'I'll have lemonade. You can keep your tea,' he told her bluntly.

She went to the larder to fill a bottle from the big crock on the stone floor. The basket would be heavy on her arm during the two-mile walk to the farm.

Now Stan appeared, still in his pyjamas, rubbing the sleep from his eyes. 'What's going on, for Pete's sake?' he demanded truculently, for he was starting a cold and felt wretched.

'I'm going with Mum,' said Tom, with irritating brevity.

'So I see,' he muttered, glancing at the pile of provisions on the table. His mother's eyes were pleading with him to say nothing, to accept the situation over which they had no control. Stan was sorry for her, but immensely relieved that he wouldn't be left all day with Tom. He slid round the table to stand on the hearthrug to warm his hands at the blazing fire and Annie smiled at her first-born, for she knew and understood his relief. Her smile was warm and tender. She seemed to be saying – 'Don't worry, Stan, I'll manage.' Her work-roughened hand stroked his cheek. It was such a simple gesture but it was enough to satisfy him.

17

Tom was standing there with his up-lifted, listening face. He did not need to be comforted or reassured for he was self-sufficient, but for the dog.

Now Annie was putting on her hat and coat and they were ready to leave.

'I'll do the vegetables for supper and I'll have the tea ready when you get back,' Stan promised. 'So long, Mum. So long, Tom.'

It was the first time they had walked together in the street, and when Tom slipped his arm into hers, Annie was a little embarrassed and apprehensive. He did not drag on her arm and seemed to rely more on the dog for guidance. Stan had made a harness for Ben from strips of soft leather with a leash attached, so there was no more straining and panting. The basket soon began to weigh heavily on her arm but Annie made no mention of it, for she was accustomed to carrying heavy baskets of washing. She was surprised at the brisk pace for she had expected they would walk very slowly and had been worried about being late on the first day of picking.

The early morning freshness was pleasing to a woman who had never slept late in her life. 'It's the best time of day,' she told Tom, for she was determined they would not walk in silence all the way to the farm.

'You may be right,' he conceded grudgingly, and added, 'Stan didn't want me to come.'

'He was surprised. You could have mentioned it last night.'

'I only thought of it this morning when I heard you go downstairs soon after the church clock struck five.'

'You can hear the church clock?'

'Yes, quite distinctly. I often hear it in the night when I can't sleep.'

She turned her head to look at him with her dark, sorrowing eyes. She hadn't known that he lay awake while his

18

brother slept soundly in his own bed. There was so much she had still to learn about her blinded boy. If only she could be sure that he really needed her, that his mother was the person to whom he would turn if his own dark little world became too unbearable to endure. Was it too late to make that close contact a mother naturally expects with a handicapped child? But Tom was a grown man and repulsed all her attempts at a close relationship. There they were, the three of them, obliged to live together for years, perhaps for always, since Stan and Tom would not marry and the strain was telling on their nerves. If only Tom would co-operate and accept a little help in the right spirit, it could be so different. The two brothers could have helped each other, for Stan was still missing the quaint child he had married and lost in such tragic circumstances. Even the Boy Scouts could not entirely compensate for Kathie. Yet they had to admire Tom for his courage and determination, for he never whined or complained when things went wrong or he cracked his head on some hard obstacle. He swore loudly and lustily! They no longer spoke of 'poor Tom' for he defied such a pitying label.

'We shan't be late after all,' Annie reflected as they reached the far boundary of the farm's spreading acres.

But Tom made no answer. He was listening for familiar sounds, sniffing the earthy smells, his face alight with the excitement of returning to this well-remembered territory of his boyhood. Tom had known exactly what he wanted to be when he left the village school as the age of fourteen – a farm-hand, at Brook's farm.

'It smells good, Mum,' he said, and now she knew for certain where he belonged, even in his blindness. They had made a mistake in thinking to protect him. To provide shelter and food and a safe little place in which to work was not enough, not for Tom. But what could he do on a farm? Wouldn't he be just an added responsibility to an over-worked farmer and his wife?

But Tom had stopped at the open gate of the farmyard and Ben was barking excitedly. Surely he could not remember his birthplace?

'Well, look who's here!' cried a cheery voice from the open door. 'Jim! It's Tom – yes, Tom Parsons.' Mrs Brook hurried across the yard, drying her hands on a white apron. She cupped Tom's face in her hands and kissed him as naturally as she kissed her own two sons before the war had robbed her of both. Seeing Tom brought it all back in a rush of memory for the three boys had shared many a happy hour together in the farm kitchen when the day's work was done. The two mothers exchanged a glance of sympathetic understanding, while Tom blushed with surprise and pleasure at the unexpected embrace.

'It's good to see you, Tom – and you, Mrs Parsons. We only meet at hop-picking time, don't we? But how quickly it comes round.'

'Good morning, Mrs Brook. How are you?' Tom was asking politely.

'Can't grumble. Just the old trouble with the bronchitis every winter, but it comes and goes – like the seasons, eh, Tom?'

He knew about Dan and Brian, and they all were remembering those two lively boys in the momentary silence. He would miss them sadly in the hop garden. They all had been crazy on the horses – the two magnificent Shires, Prince and Duke, and the two mares, Nancy and Kitty.

'Hello, Tom!' the gruff familiar voice greeted him, and his hand was grasped in a firm grip. 'Nice to see you, lad. It's been a long time. You've grown a few inches and put on quite a lot of weight since we last met, but you were always a strong, sturdy lad. Nice to see you back, Mrs Parsons. The hops look good this year and should make for easy picking. Five bushels to the shilling seems a fair price.'

20

It was a standing joke. Every year he repeated the same prediction for the benefit of his pickers, but when they moved into the lower garden where the hops were small, the gypsies and Cockneys would demand a better rate. So they laughed, and Tom joined in the laughter, his face still glowing with the pleasure of meeting his friendly employers of pre-war days.

'You've still got Ben, I see.'

The dog was pawing at the farmer's breeches.

'What's this? You training him for the circus ring, Tom?'

'I'm training him to lead, Mr Brook. He's darn good. We take walks together across the fields at the back of the house. Don't we, Mum?'

'Yes, that's right,' Annie agreed, smiling proudly at her son.

'A dog is a wonderful companion, and Ben was the best of Sally's litter that year, I remember,' Mr Brook was saying.

Now they could hear the noisy bedlam of the Cockney families in the huts down the lane, and a few minutes later the bellowing voice of old Harry Stone echoed across the nearest hop-garden, 'All to work!'

'Come on, Mum,' said Tom, urging the dog forward. 'Let's get started!'

The three who had eyes to see the grace and beauty of those long, green arches before picking started gazed after the sturdy figure. There was no need to take his mother's arm. Why, he knew every inch of the way! Stumbling over the hard clods, his face brushed by overhanging branches of hops, Tom followed the dog with an eagerness reflected in the wide grin. Annie hurried after him, expecting to see him trip and fall, but neither the clods of earth nor the branches seemed to worry him. He could hear the clamour of the Cockney families gathering at the lower end of the

21

garden, the barking of dogs, and the raucous voices of frantic Mums whose off-spring had already strayed.

'Maudie! – Alfie! – Charlie!'

Tom could see it all in retrospect – the reluctant kids, suspicious of the bins they saw lined up and that authoritative shout of Harry's – 'All to work' – were sneaking away through the gaps in the hedges. Once upon a time he and his brothers had escaped from the irksome task of picking hops into a bin, but not on the first day when it was still a novelty, with the promise of pennies to spend at the end of the week and a visit to Tunbridge Wells when all the gardens were stripped, to buy their winter boots and overcoats. Stan and Dick had plodded on gamely, hour after hour, with only brief dashes to a nearby wood. Gordon had complained of heat and scratches and feeling sick, so had often been excused to lie in the shade. As for his own good intentions to earn enough to buy those winter boots, Tom had to admit he was the first to tire, the first to suggest the re-filling of the water bottle at the farmyard tap, the first to demand 'something to eat' – and the last back after the dinner hour!

'This way, Tom,' his mother was calling. She had recognised several of the 'home-pickers' gathered around the set of bins, separated from the rest, as always. The segregation of the pickers could not have been more pronounced than the segregation of the three distinct classes of society in the village – Cockneys, gypsies and home-pickers assembled on that first morning, the mothers anxious to start on the picking, the children staring boldly or shyly, according to the nature of their tribe.

Annie was greeted civilly by all the women in her set – women who had grown old and grey in the long years since Annie first struggled with the pramcart over the rough clods – women with sad eyes whose husbands and sons had not come home when the war was over. The children stared

22

curiously at Tom, a little puzzled by his attitude and Mrs Parsons' guiding hand on her son's arm. Some remembered him vaguely, but it was a long time ago when he was a boy, and now he was a man.

Then one little girl, in a long pinafore and button boots, ran forward to pat the dog. Soon they were surrounded by the children, all clamouring to pat Ben, asking questions without embarrassment now that one mother had explained in a hoarse whisper, 'Tom's blind – he can't see.'

Now it was Tom and not the dog receiving all the attention. He was led to the empty bin that had been reserved for his mother and sat carefully down on its wooden edge. They could hardly wait to see him start picking.

'How will you know if you are picking hops or leaves?' a boy demanded.

Tom was still grinning. 'I can feel, can't I?' he reminded them.

'Can you feel me?' asked the little girl standing close beside him.

Tom ran his hands over her and she stood quite still while he pronounced, 'This is your pinafore. This is your sunbonnet – and this funny little object must be your nose!'

Then she giggled delightedly and was pushed away.

'Feel me!'

'No, me!' they clamoured, but were quickly collected by the anxious mothers.

'You mustn't worry Tom,' they said, but Tom was not at all disturbed by the children, only impatient to start picking from the bine that Annie had hung over his knees.

While she stood at the other end of the bine, stripping off the hops with practised skill, he groped for them among the leaves with his clumsy fingers. Ben lay quietly at his feet.

Two hours had passed quickly. The babble of voices had dwindled to a hum, a baby cried, a dog barked. It was very pleasant in the garden, Tom was thinking, his face lifted to

23

catch the warm rays of the sun as it filtered through the gap where the bines had been pulled. He was happy and relaxed, and he spoke to his mother in a bantering way about the leaves that were falling into the bin. It was true and Annie was dismayed, for she was a clean picker. With Tom looking so pleased with himself she could not spoil his pleasure, so she leaned over the bin repeatedly to pick out the leaves.

When the farmer came their way, after his routine inspection of the garden and the pickers, he quickly noted the situation from the shade of the bines where he stood watching the mother and son for some moments. 'That poor little woman. She can't spend six weeks picking out Tom's leaves,' he was thinking.

'How's it going, Tom lad?' he called out, then he stepped forward, peered into the bin and whistled. 'Not bad,' he conceded, 'but not good enough for your mother, eh, Mrs Parsons?'

Annie blushed uncomfortably and insisted, 'I don't mind picking out the leaves, Mr Brook.'

'Tell you what we'll do, Tom. We'll divide the bin into two halves with this twine. You remember, you boys used to pick in separate halves once you were old enough to have your own tally books.'

Tom was standing up, frowning anxiously now and feeling rather foolish. His lifted face had clouded, his mouth was twitching. How quickly the lad took offence.

The farmer gripped Tom's shoulders. 'I've got a better idea,' he said heartily. 'You can pull the bines for this set and give Harry a rest. He's not so young any more and his heart is a bit groggy. The kids can come and fetch you when their Mums are ready for more bines to be pulled. I'll tell Harry you are taking over. It will give you a break from picking and you'll be doing me a favour lad, for we are still short-handed and likely to be, I'm thinking,

24

for a long time ahead.'

Tom knew he was speaking of his own two sons as well as young Steve Webber – all lying in the unfriendly earth of a foreign field. Tom was too concerned with his own immediate future to spare much time for the friends who would never come home.

'Thanks! Thanks Mr Brook. I'll be glad to help,' he said. And now he was smiling again.

It was a grand diversion for the home-pickers' children, and Tom could hear their shrill voices demanding, 'It's my turn to fetch Tom!' 'It's not fair, Mum. She fetched him last time!'

Ben was getting a little worried and confused by all the scampering about, for he was told to lie still like a good dog. However, he was rewarded in the dinner hour when Tom fed him titbits from his own dinner, filled his tin bowl with fresh water and announced, 'Walk, Ben!' He led the way down a straight green archway and Tom's tuneless whistle floated back to Annie as she sipped her second cup of tea from the flask. Now all her doubts of having him with her in the hop garden had drifted away, and they both would enjoy the six weeks in the fresh air and sunshine, as well as the agreeable company of the other pickers.

A few minutes after Harry's resounding call 'All to work!', Tom was back at the bine with the dog. The afternoon hours seemed long and tiring that first day, with the sun hot on their backs. Mothers were cross with children who had stayed too long in the woods and pretended not to hear that 'All to work!' when it had echoed round the acres as clearly as a bell.

'I can hear the wagon,' said Tom, in the late afternoon, 'that means they are starting on the second measuring – Mr Brook and Harry.' He sighed with longing for the days before the war, when he was part of the team of men and horses collecting the hops to be dried in the oasts. It was a long time ago, that last summer before the war, when he was a lad of sixteen, without a care in the world. Then he heard the farmer calling authoritatively, 'Tom! Hey, Tom! Give us a hand here, will you lad? Harry's feeling the heat. You, Jimmy, go and fetch Tom, there's a good boy.'

And Tom found himself back in 1913, holding up a sack while the hops poured in from the bushel basket, ' – four – five – six – seven' Mrs Bond and her old mother had not wasted a moment, and now they looked pleased and well satisfied with the total of bushels in the tally book for the first day's picking. The neighbours were waiting their turn, for competition was keen among the home-pickers. The acrid smell of sulphur was sweeter in Tom's nostrils than the sweetest scent, and he tied the twine round the neck of the bulging sack with a practised skill that had not been forgotten.

Now they were moving on to the first set of Cockney pickers and young Jim was his guide. The respectful home-pickers had stood aside politely while the farmer measured their hops, but the Cockney families crowded about the bins, watching suspiciously.

'Gahn! That was too full that last one, Mister. You ain't 'arf stingy,' a loud voice complained, while her kids added their own grumbles in her defence.

'Gahn! Be a sport, Mister!'

Tom's grinning face was lifted expectantly for he had always enjoyed this battle of the bins between farmer and pickers. Farmer Brook made light of all the complaints and remained as good-humoured as ever in the barrage of abuse.

'Watcher been doing with yerself then, Tom?' Granny Smith demanded. She stank of beer and stale sweat. 'You caught a proper packet an' no mistake. Them bloody 'uns as a lot ter answer for one of these days, an' Purgatory's too

26

good for that lot of bastards!' Granny Smith was a devout Catholic, and knew all about Purgatory.

Tom's red face turned a deeper shade of red as he stood there surrounded by their curious stares, but they were just being kind. This was their way. He liked and understood the Cockneys, but disliked and distrusted the Gypsies. Then a sticky toffee was pushed in his hand and a small voice asked, 'Can't you see nuffink then?'

'Nuffink!' he told her, with a wide grin that defied pity.

'You ain't 'arf clever.'

Her childish praise pleased Tom enormously. He wanted to hug her, for he was beginning to feel an affinity with children he did not feel with adults. Dogs and children accepted him in his blindness.

'Give Tom a kiss, Katie. Go on, Luv. Give 'im a nice kiss,' her mother urged.

And Katie stood on tiptoe and obligingly pressed her sticky mouth to Tom's.

'Thank you, Katie,' he said gratefully, while the counting continued, uninterrupted by such small incidences.

'Two, – three – four,' the children chanted.

'Gahn! You left another bushel in the bin!' a boy shouted indignantly.

'Not even half,' the farmer told him – and moved on to the next bin.

A young woman in her early twenties had been watching Tom in mingled surprise and admiration, but she did not speak when Jimmy brought him close to the bin she was sharing with a younger sister. A fourteen-year-old girl had plenty of cheek, so she left her to do all the talking. She was standing so close to Tom the blank stare of eyes that once had flattered her seemed to be looking directly into her own eyes.

'Don't mess me abaht. I don't let no feller mess me abaht,' she had warned him when he did no more than touch her bare arm. 'I seen too much of it with me own Mum and Dad on Sat'day nights ter last me a lifetime,' she had explained.

In spite of his red hair and quick temper, Tom had been patient and understanding, she remembered. Even on their last evening together in the oast he had stolen only one kiss.

'So long, Tom! See yer next 'opping!' she had yelled from the crowded doorway of the departing train. She was fifteen and Tom was sixteen. It was a long time ago, but now it seemed she had lived another life since that summer of 1913. She hadn't been able to keep her virginity with the streets and pubs swarming with soldiers and sailors of every nationality. All the girls at the munitions factory had stories to tell of the fun they were having, and she hadn't wanted to be different from the rest. Making love in dark alleyways wasn't a lot of fun, she soon discovered. It wasn't love at all. It was just the same old 'messing abaht' that had so disgusted her when she shared the communal bedroom with her parents, and cowered under dirty blankets covering her ears; but one had wanted to marry her and the girls said she would be a fool to refuse such an offer, for she would get his Army allowance and live in Canada after the war. She was not at all sure about going to live in Canada with a man she hardly knew. The East End was her home. She was a Londoner born and bred, but as it happened, it wasn't required of her to pull up her roots, for the Canadian corporal was killed a few weeks after slipping the ring on her finger. She was still wearing the ring. Why not? She was married, wasn't she?

Now she found she was near to tears, and she hadn't cried not even when Mum followed Dad to the cemetery in the 'flu epidemic after the war. So she moved away from the sturdy figure of the man she had known as a boy. She could not bear to watch the light and the shadow on his lifted, listening face.

A week had passed, and still she hesitated. Tom's mother had not recognised her, and when the farmer came their way morning and afternoon with his bushel basket, escorted by Tom and young Jimmy, she stood back in the archway and left her sister with the tally-book. If the farmer remembered a courtship that summer before the war, he gave no sign, but merely lifted his hand in salute and moved on to the next bin. It was unusual to find a Cockney female with nothing to say for herself, but perhaps she was embarrassed by Tom's sightless eyes. Some were, some weren't. As far as he and his wife were concerned, they found Tom still the same likable lad and just as willing to help as when he had two good eyes. He was making a good job of pulling the bines, helping to shift the bins, and hadn't lost the knack of holding up the sack at measuring time. They all had held their breath that first day, when Tom had followed the dog on its straining leash to the stationary wagon. With utter fearlessness he had approached those two great Shires in the shafts of the wagon, reaching out his hand till he felt the solid bulk of a broad back. Annie had gasped, 'Tom! Take care!' but the farmer had reassured her.

'He's all right, Prince and Duke will remember him. Wait and see.'

Now an audience had gathered at a safe distance, and mothers shushed their children who watched with fascinated curiosity. Tom was their hero now.

'Crikey!' whispered the young Cockneys. 'Tom ain't 'arf brave.'

They held their breath again when he took an apple from his pocket and offered it to the leading horse on the palm of his hand. The enormous mouth opened, the apple disappeared and the children let out their breath, for Tom's

29

hand was still there! The second horse received its apple in the same way, standing perfectly still, though the dog barked excitedly round the huge shaggy hooves. Tom was talking to the horses, but they could not hear what he was saying. The children welcomed this further diversion twice a day, and gathered in little groups as soon as the wagon rumbled across the garden. If Tom was showing off for their benefit, he deserved to be noticed and admired.

Among his twice-daily audience was the quiet young woman in her ill-fitting, second-hand clothes from the stall in the street market. She was thin and her features were sharp, but her eyes were still as bright as a squirrel's in her peaked face. She was not normally so quiet and subdued, for she could be the life and soul of any party in the local pub when she felt like it. 'Come on, Rube – give us a song!' they would say – and somebody would bash the keys of the old joanna. It was usually one of Marie Lloyd's, for Marie was a great favourite and they never tired of hearing her songs. Ruby was a scream they said, and her imitations so lifelike, you really wouldn't know the difference.

'You ought ter go on the stage, Rube,' they said. 'You'd make a packet.'

'Gahn! Don't talk so daft!' she told them. What would they say if they could see her now? She hardly knew what to make of herself as she watched and waited for a glimpse of that manly figure in breeches, plaid shirt and heavy gum-boots. He looked, and was, still the same healthy young animal. His shoulders were broad, his chest hairy, his face scorched by the sun, his hair a carroty red. This was Tom, the boy she had not forgotten in all the troubled years since they last met. This was Tom, grown to manhood, and she was shy of him because he could not see her.

'What's the matter with you, Rube? You sick or something?' her young sister had demanded irritably. 'It used to be more fun in the old days when we come 'opping with

30

Mum and the boys,' she reminded Ruby. But Nellie was only a kid, and she had escaped all the 'messing abaht' in dark alleyways during the war – but only just, for at thirteen she had a bust she was proud to display, while Ruby's chest was flat. It was going to be an impossible situation now that Nellie had finished school, and would be starting work as a waitress in a café as soon as hop-picking was over. Already she defied her elder sister and ran the streets after school, chasing the boys down those same dark alleyways that had seen so much kissing and cuddling in the past.

'You mind yer own blinkin' business Rube, an' I'll mind mine.'

What could you do with a girl who spoke so disrespectful? Ruby asked herself repeatedly these days.

Now she had this new anxiety, that saddened and confused her. There was no telling from day to day whether she would speak to Tom or let him pass. Why couldn't she take the initiative and break this spell of silence and shyness that his blindness had imposed on her? A week had slipped away, and every day she kept her mouth shut when he was standing there, quite unconscious of her nearness. What would his reactions be if she spoke? Perhaps he would be puzzled for he may have forgotten that girl who hadn't wanted to be 'messed abaht'. After all, they hadn't slept together. They hadn't removed any of their clothes in the warm oasthouse. Just one kiss, as pure and chaste as though she had been kissing a brother. Had Tom been disappointed that last evening? She wondered now why he hadn't forced her for he was so strong and sturdy, and she so small and skinny. Yet she couldn't bear it if he had forgotten her, if she had to remind him of those stolen hours in the oast, when his work on the farm was finished. She couldn't bear to watch his face go blank. 'Ruby? Ruby Foster? Who's she?' That would be the end for she would not speak to him again – this man who was no stranger, but

31

so strange in his blindness she was afraid to hurt him even more than she was afraid to be hurt by him.

Tom had found the weekend at home rather long and tedious for they finished picking at noon on Saturday. He deliberately avoided the workshop for he had no interest in basket-making when all his senses were alerted to that other, wider sphere, two miles away. So he wandered restlessly about the house and garden, and walked across the fields beyond the boundary fence while Annie was busy with cleaning, washing, shopping and cooking in preparation for the coming week. She knew Tom was eager to be back in the hop-garden among the pickers and the friendly children. The change in him was miraculous, and she was no longer nervous of upsetting him.

'You there, Mum?' he would call. 'How about a cup of tea?'

And she would drop whatever she was doing to brew another pot of tea for the three of them. Stan had so much work on hand they saw him only for hurried meals, but Tom was always welcome to sit with him in the workshop. They hadn't much to say but it was company for both. They respected each other's privacy and Tom would call out, 'Can I come in, Stan?' He would sit on the chair, sniffing the familiar smells of oil and rubber, listening to the whirr of a sewing machine, or the hiss of escaping air from a deflated tyre, and his big hands would twitch with impatience. Stan's workshop attracted him more than his own, for it was alive with sound. What was the use of making more baskets when there was so little demand for them? By the time the materials had been paid for, there was little profit.

'The baskets are so strong they will last a lifetime,' the postmistress had explained to Annie.

It was not an article that a customer would buy more than

once, so there they hung on their hooks above the counter, gathering the dust.

There was no need to ask Tom if he had enjoyed his first week in the hop-garden, for it was evident in his expression, and the bantering tone of his voice as he pestered his mother and brother for little jobs they had always supposed he was quite incapable of. 'I can do that, Mum.' 'Let me have a go at that, Stan.' This was his constant demand during that first weekend at home. How could they refuse when he was so eager and anxious to help? Why should they deprive him of one of his few pleasures – the satisfaction of some small achievement. He wanted applause and admiration, not pity. A gasp of surprise when he succeeded or an exclamation of wonder at his cleverness was music to his sensitive soul.

The first time he brewed the tea in the big brown teapot, and arranged cups and saucers, milk jug and sugar basin on a tray, he felt so pleased with himself, and stood in the open doorway calling urgently, 'Mum! Stan! Tea's ready!'

He could hear his mother hurrying down the garden path and Stan dropped his hammer on the floor with a loud clatter. They thought he was teasing until they saw the teapot on the hob and the tray on the table.

Annie's voice was gently reproving, 'You might have scalded yourself, Tom.'

Stan exclaimed, 'It tastes as good as Mum's,' when he had sipped the hot, strong brew they all enjoyed.

'Not bad, eh?' Tom agreed. 'Just give me time and I'll be running the house single-handed! Well, perhaps I'll let you do the washing and ironing, Mum, and I don't fancy black-leading the stove or scrubbing the scullery floor, or cleaning out the privy, but I could manage the rest.'

They laughed at his boasting and loved him for his change of heart. The bitterness and frustration must show itself from time to time, for this was inevitable, but to feel

33

his response to their combined efforts to please him was more than they had dared to hope.

'Let me help.'

Now they were hindered in their own work while he fumbled clumsily at all the little jobs they would prefer to do themselves. Their patience remedied Tom's impatience, their quietness fostered his noisy fretfulness. Tom's hands were big and broad, Stan's hands were small and narrow. The brothers were so different in feature and character the only bond between them was the blood relationship – but that could be said of all four brothers.

Annie had baked another bread pudding, a fruit cake, sausage rolls and meat patties. The basket would hang heavy on her arm again on the outward journey, but light on the homeward journey. It didn't matter. Nothing mattered only that Tom should enjoy these long days outdoors.

'I'd carry that basket for you, Mum, if I had another hand!' he told her as they started out together that second Monday morning, with Ben setting the pace.

'When you boys were little I used to say I could do with another eye in the back of my head!' said Annie – and stopped short, conscious of her mistake. Three eyes, indeed, and her poor boy with none! She glanced at his face in quick anxiety, but it had not clouded. She could not know that all his senses were straining towards that exciting moment when they passed the farmyard and he called 'Hello!' to anyone who happened to be around. It could be Mary-Ann, filling the buckets at the pump, or Mrs Brook feeding the hens, or Lizzie fetching a can of milk from the dairy, or the farmer himself, with the dogs at his heels.

'Hello, Tom!'

Some days only one voice answered, another time it was several, and Tom recognised each one, and told his mother. He was like a little boy again, waiting for praise and approval. The sense of smell, the sense of touch, the sense of hearing – all these senses had developed in the past year, and all were acutely sensitive now.

'Can you hear that reaper in the cornfield, Mum?'

'Can you hear that skylark?'

No, Annie could not hear, so they would stop and listen.

'Now I can hear it, Tom,' she would say.

But he was not satisfied to hear it once. He had to stop every day to listen to the same reaper, the same skylark, like a child who wants to have the same story repeated.

'Can you smell the silage, Mum?'

'Yes, it's horrid.'

'It smells good to me.'

'Does it, Tom?'

'When you find another hop-dog in the bin, let me have it, Mum. I want to hold it.'

The 'hop-dogs' were fluffy brown caterpillars, and Annie shuddered as she picked them out of the bin.

They were drawing closer together, now, mother and son, day by day, but would it last when the hop-picking season was over, Annie asked herself? She tried not to worry; there were five more weeks to enjoy the fresh air and sunshine, and the lively company that surrounded them all the long day.

Now Tom had finished his dinner and was following Ben down the green archway. Half of the dinner hour had already passed, and he must be back at the bin when Harry called 'All to work!' For his mother's sake he must not linger on that sunny bank at the far end of the gardens. She worried about him when he was out of sight in case he would meet with an accident. Yet he felt so safe in this place where he still belonged – safe and happy. If only the hop-picking season would last and he hadn't to go back to that cramped little hut in the garden, and the baskets that nobody wanted to buy. Perhaps something would happen and he need not go back?

'Oh, God – let something happen!'

A branch brushed his face. He could hear the shrill voices of Cockney children in the woods. The gypsy children slipped past, furtive as little foxes. ''E can't see us,' they whispered – no, but he could hear!

The young woman in the ill-fitting, shabby clothes, unwashed face and hair, and torn stockings followed Tom and the dog at a safe distance. At the end of the green archway she saw him sitting on the bank with the dog between his knees, his face lifted in the warmth of the sun. She was still shy of him, still confused by those sightless eyes, yet drawn to him, against her will, by some compelling force. She wanted to escape, to have nothing more to do with this man who was so like the boy she had known in that Summer before the war.

When she followed him down the green archway, she saw that he squared his broad shoulders and strode along with his head up and she was amazed at his fearlessness. His red hair seemed to be afire in the strong sunlight, but his red face had clouded. What was troubling him? She was choked with tears and longing to run away, but her boots seemed to be glued to the clods, and she could not move. Now it was too late to wish she had gone with Nellie to pinch apples in the orchard.

'Gahn! You're scared!' her sister had jeered. It was too late, because the dog had seen her.

In that same instant Tom had also sensed an intruder and both were wary, resenting a third party in their favourite haunt.

'Who's there?' Tom demanded, and Ben barked sharply.

There was no answer.

'Who is it? Why don't you answer?' Tom repeated irritably.

'It's me – Ruby, Ruby Foster.' Her voice was husky in her tight throat, and she shivered in the shade of the over-hanging branches. The cloud lifted from his listening face as a veil is lifted, and the wide grin likened him still more to the boy she once knew.

'Ruby!' he shouted exultantly. 'For God's sake, where have you sprung from? Come here! Let me feel you.' He stretched his hands towards her and the dog barked again. 'Quiet, Ben. It's a friend – an old friend,' he said sooth-ingly. Then his big hands closed over hands that were so small and the wrists so thin he thought they would snap. He tightened his grip for fear she would disappear as suddenly and mysteriously as she had arrived.

'Say something! Have you lost your tongue?' He was trembling with excitement, laughing and crying. He could smell the hops on her clothes, and it delighted him more than the costliest scent. He could feel the vibration in their clasped hands, hear her quick panting breath. But it was not enough. He wanted to see her. God! Why couldn't he see her? Now the tears streamed from those sightless eyes, and she fell on her knees and cradled his head to her breast, her skinny arms like a vice about his neck.

'Oh, Tom – oh, duckie,' she sobbed, her own tears wet on her cheeks.

In that moment of watching him from the archway, she had slipped off her wedding ring. She had no use for it now. She knew exactly what she was going to do. Searching for a handkerchief, Ruby remembered the piece of rag she had tucked into her knicker elastic. It was grubby and sticky, and she looked at it in shame and dismay and tucked it back in her drawers.

Tom was reaching for a handkerchief too, in the pocket of his plaid shirt. It was clean and starched, and neatly folded. His Mum was looking after him properly. She could see a neat patch on the knee of his breeches, and she

37

wondered what his Mum would say to a Cockney daughter-in-law.

Tom was wiping her face with the clean handkerchief, then he wiped his own face. They both smelled of hops and sweat. They both had a thousand questions to ask, but they could wait.

When Tom had pushed the handkerchief back in his pocket, he asked humbly, pleadingly, 'Will you let me feel you since I can't see you?'

She was surprised at his gentleness, and made no protest when his fumbling fingers unbuttoned her blouse. With a little shiver of acquiescence she knelt there on the grassy bank while he cupped her breasts as gently as he had cupped her cheeks. Then he sighed, fastened the buttons and hugged her tightly. He was holding her now between his knees, and they both had forgotten the dog till he barked to remind them, for he was puzzled and suspicious of his master's behaviour.

'Ben! It's all right, boy. Come, then,' Tom invited – and they made room for him, laughing at his wet kisses and his fanning, feathery tail.

'Your dog likes me, Tom,' said Ruby nervously, for she had never known the company of a dog, or any animal but mice in the crowded tenement.

'All to work!'

It echoed round the garden, and they both knew they could not refuse to obey that summons, for they were not free to please themselves. They walked back hand-in-hand down the cool, green arches, with Ben setting the pace.

Chapter Two

When Linda walked in only three months after reporting back to the Field Hospital in France, she found Dick comfortably installed in the sitting-room of their private flat, in the west wing of the school. The table was piled with exercise books and the red pencil still in his hand when he sprang to his feet, exclaiming, 'Linda! My dear, what are you doing here?'

'Hello,' she said casually, snatching off her hat.

Dick helped her off with her coat.

'Well, you haven't wasted any time in getting established. I congratulate you, Dick,' she said, with a hint of patronage.

Dick smiled with kindly tolerance. She was tired after the long journey, and upset – but why was she upset? In the few short weeks he had known Linda intimately, he had accepted that she was moody and temperamental – 'highly strung' his mother would call this new daughter-in-law she had not yet met. Dick pushed her gently into an armchair, took a cigarette from the packet she had left behind in their honeymoon hotel bedroom in her hurried dash for the station, and lit it for her. Soon she leaned back, her body relaxed, and he bent to kiss her pale tense face.

'I'm your husband, remember?' he reminded her, quietly.

'That's why I'm here. I am going to have your child, Dick – and I don't want a child,' she told him, her dark eyes accusing.

He stared at her in amazed satisfaction at his own virility. He had fathered a child!

'But my dear, that's wonderful,' he said, and kissed her mouth. Her lips were cool and she did not return the kiss. She was tired and upset, he reminded himself again, but there was something more tangible than fretfulness in those dark eyes. It was open hostility and dislike.

'What's so wonderful about it? Aren't there enough little brats in this place without having one of our own?'

Dick had no answer to such an unkind question, for he was too shocked and surprised. He thought it was natural that a woman should want children.

'Didn't we promise each other to be honest and to have no secrets? Well, I am being honest with you now. I am not the maternal type, Dick, and I was pretty disgusted, I don't mind telling you, when I discovered I was pregnant. Why didn't you stop me? I get excited. You should have had more sense. Aren't you supposed to be the dominant partner? Sexual intercourse was not primarily instituted for the begetting of children. That's an old-fashioned conception. It was my mistake not to discuss it with you before marriage. It's too late now.' She sighed and yawned expansively. 'Make me some coffee, will you, Dick – black and strong. I feel awful.'

She closed her eyes and he felt he was dismissed. He had been sitting at her feet, his thin sensitive face flushed with embarrassment. He was not the dominant partner and she knew it. She had taken him on their wedding night and subsequently during that short honeymoon, for she was not content to wait for the darkness of night to cover their nakedness, but delighted in their nakedness at every opportunity during the daylight hours. It had been an exhausting and devastating experience. He remembered lying with her in the heart of a beech wood, in which the silence was broken only by the scampering of a curious squirrel along the branches, and the rustling of rabbits in the bracken. It was a peaceful, pleasant place for lovers, yet her sensuality had spoiled it. He hadn't the physical strength or the right mentality to cope with such an over-sexed woman, yet he admired and loved her.

He stood there, looking down at her with questioning eyes. What did the future hold? It was only the beginning of their married life and already it was threatened by Linda's unwillingness to bear children. He could not understand why she had accepted the post of Matron in her cousin's preparatory school if she disliked children. This joint appointment had seemed like a heaven-sent opportunity to Dick, with so many ex-servicemen looking for jobs. In a country environment far removed from the sickness and suffering in the cruel aftermath of war, they could build a new life for themselves. But could they, Dick was asking himself as he went to the kitchen to put on the kettle?

This flat was home now, and he had enjoyed the past few weeks of his first term once he had conquered his initial shyness and apprehension. Roger had welcomed him warmly, the boys had accepted him with typical schoolboy tolerance. A new master was a novelty and a target for their pranks. On the whole they liked his quiet authority. It was a change to have a master who did not raise his voice or use the cane. A serious offender was sent to the Head to be caned, but Dick Parsons would never be an idol or a hero to his pupils, since he played neither cricket nor football, and even to sprint a few yards across the playing fields left him gasping for breath.

'You all right, sir?' they would ask, anxiously crowding about him.

'Golly, sir, you do look whacked.'

They were likable little lads and Dick had settled down nicely in his new role. Now his confidence was badly shaken, and he brewed the coffee with a sense of foreboding in a future that had seemed so bright and promising.

'Dick and his wife are coming home for Christmas,' said Annie, in shiny-eyed expectancy.

'Coming here?' Stan seemed surprised.

'Dick will be coming here and his wife will be staying with her father.'

'Good.' Stan usually spoke bluntly and he was nothing if not honest. They both were relieved at the arrangement, yet, at the same time, aware of its strangeness. Surely a husband and wife should want to spend Christmas together?

Annie always referred to her daughter-in-law as 'Dick's wife' and still avoided Dr Pearce. How could she ever be familiar with this superior young woman who had married Dick when she had always been known as 'Miss Linda' in the village? Now she read the remainder of the letter and gasped at the last paragraph.

'She's expecting! Dick's wife is expecting!'

'Is she?' Stan went on eating his breakfast. Memories of that other pregnancy and its disastrous consequences were suddenly renewed in all their poignancy.

'But why does he keep the most important news till last?' his mother was asking. Stan was not listening, so she did not repeat the question. The bright moment of pleasure was already fading in the unresponsive face across the table, and she looked at her firstborn and understood. She, too, remembered the shock and the suffering they had shared, and her own sense of personal loss, for she had loved young Kathie as her own daughter, and longed to hold a baby in her arms again.

When she had poured another cup of tea for Stan, and waited for the sad mood to pass, she went on talking about the expected child with gentle insistence, for she had to share it with someone, and only Stan was left at home now.

He was a good son, and no mother could ask for one better. He lived for his work and the Boy Scouts, so they met only for meals, and she had got into the habit of telling him all that was on her mind in rather a hurry.

'That explains it, of course,' she went on chattily. 'Dick's wife would want to go to her own home because the old nurse is the housekeeper now. She came back to look after the doctor and she's still there. Won't she be pleased about this baby? I wonder if she has kept any of the baby clothes? I kept all mine. There is sure to be a lovely christening robe, for that is something handed down from one generation to another in better-class families. You all were wrapped in a shawl, but it was a very nice shawl, and with careful washing is still as good as new. Anyway, an old nurse should have plenty of good advice for a young wife expecting her first child.'

'Perhaps she doesn't need advice. She always seemed a very self-possessed young woman, though I haven't seen her since before the war,' Stan suggested, since his mother seemed to expect him to show a little interest in his prospective niece or nephew.

'I expect she will want everything new for the baby, but she's welcome to borrow all my baby clothes for there they are, in that cupboard, all nicely washed, starched and ironed.' Her voice trailed away, for they both knew the clothes had been waiting for Stan's baby – only it wasn't Stan's baby. It was Gordon's. After a while she spoke again.

'I hope it's a little girl,' she said wistfully.

Stan agreed, then pushed back his chair and went out of the room, leaving her sitting there, with both joy and sadness in her motherly heart. She was still sitting there with the letter in her hand when Stan came back to say, in a sudden, inexplicable confidence, 'By the way, Mum, I've found out where Gordon is living. One of these days I'll

43

look him up and tell him he can come home if he likes. After all, it's a long time ago, and maybe he wasn't entirely to blame for what happened.'

Before Annie could switch her thoughts from her first grandchild to her youngest son, Stan was back in the workshop. Now what had prompted him to that change of heart? And where had he discovered Gordon's hideout?

Life was still surprising and children as unpredictable as ever. One door closed and another opened. Tom had left home. Was Gordon coming back?

It was quite by chance that Stan had traced Gordon's movements after he left home, and he had intended to follow up the clue, but had been too busy. A few more weeks could make little difference, and he was not exactly anxious to meet his young brother again. His conscience had been bothering him for some time, however. A Scout leader should set a good example to the boys, and to harbour such bitterness and resentment was not in keeping with the fine principles of the movement. At one time he would have given Gordon such a thrashing as he would never have forgotten. He could have killed him in a fit of ungovernable rage, for Gordon had no defence against punishment, other than tears and a plea for mercy like a frightened child; but that madness had passed long since, for Stan was a gentle soul by nature and the most like his mother. He was also slow to act and his impulses lacked the energy and initiative of his brothers.

The two absorbing occupations, work and Scouting, left no time for anything else. He was a good son, as Annie was the first to admit, but something vital and necessary to his manhood and mentality had died with Kathie, and never been replaced. Stan had found a vocation in the boys, and it sufficed and satisfied.

44

They had followed their usual plan that Saturday, before the start of the hop-picking season, and set out for the woods as soon as the lads had finished their various little jobs that earned a few shillings towards the fund. Stan had taken the precaution to get permission from the owner of the estate to camp in the woods and to light a fire in a clearing. It had everything that was necessary to their enjoyment, including a running stream of fresh water and trees to climb. In the surrounding acres dead branches and twigs could be gathered to feed the fire. They could boil a kettle and fry bread and potatoes in the blackened old frying pan. They were busy as bees in their favourite haunt, and the hours slipped away most pleasantly, or had done so on previous occasions.

On this particular Saturday, the rain persisted, and the sky was heavy with clouds. In the true tradition of Boy Scouts they refused to be defeated in their plans and set forth manfully with loaded haversacks and high spirits, draped in the rubberised ground-sheets they had purchased for their camping holiday.

'It's looking brighter over there, sir,' said one, pointing to a strip of light in the threatening clouds.

'Our Mum always says rain before seven, clear up before eleven,' piped another helpfully.

'But it's going on for twelve now and still raining,' the only doubtful member of the troop pointed out. He was alone in his pessimism.

They sang as they marched along, their boots squelching in mud and puddles, their stiffened hat brims – so carefully pressed for the routine inspection of uniforms – soon soggy with water, their fresh young faces glowing and glistening in the rain.

By the time they reached the outskirts of the wood it was obvious to even the most optimistic that it was no sort of weather for camping. Everything was drenched. Dripping branches added further discomfort, and when the eldest and most resourceful boy in the troop actually admitted it would be quite impossible to light a fire, the rest stood around drooping with disappointment.

Then Stan remembered the gamekeeper's cottage. They had passed it a number of times and the boys had peered through the windows.

'We could shelter there, if we can get inside, but it's probably locked,' he suggested.

The wet faces brightened instantly, and they hurried towards the cottage in the track of their worried leader, whose own spirits had been kept from flagging by the energy and enthusiasm of the boys. Several of the bigger lads raced ahead, all wanting to be first at the cottage.

'It's not locked! The door's not locked!' they called back. 'Shall we go in, sir?' they clamoured excitedly.

It was one of those crucial moments when a leader has to make a decision and take full responsibility for the consequences. The boys stood back respectfully while Stan pushed open the door. It was dirty and dusty and stank of mice and mildew, but it seemed to the drenched youngsters who tumbled inside an abode of luxury, and they shouted with glee at their great good fortune.

'Look, sir, there's a fireplace.'

'And there's wood in the hearth, sir – dry wood!'

'Can we light a fire, sir?'

They crowded about him with shining, eager faces.

'Yes, you can light a fire, but if the chimney smokes we must let it out. First, take off your wet capes and hats and hang them in the porch. We can't have them dripping in here.'

While they scrambled around in the porch, Stan slipped off his own belted mackintosh and hat and looked about the small crowded room for a nail on which to hang it. The walls were plastered with unframed pictures. A strange

46

hobby, he thought, for a gamekeeper?

Then his attention was caught and riveted on one particular picture, and he stood there, staring at the naked figure of his brother Gordon; a hot flush of embarrassment stained his neck and face, and he hurriedly draped the picture with the mackintosh. So this explained the mystery of Gordon's secret haunt on all those Sunday afternoons and evenings when he had refused to say where he spent his time – and they all had assumed he was meeting a girl! But it still didn't explain why a gamekeeper should want to paint a naked boy. Stan could see no beauty in nakedness, only this shameful embarrassment.

'There's no paper, sir,' a boy was standing beside him, and Stan forced his mind to concentrate on the immediate demands of these other boys – normal, decent lads, who spent their free time in the proper way. He shivered while his face still burned. This was something Stan had not encountered, even in the Army, but Dick and Tom would have known that a certain type of man can be infatuated by a pretty boy. He saw it as something indecent, obscene – a depraved form of art.

'Paper, sir – there's no paper to light the fire,' the boy persisted, staring at his leader's flushed face.

'Try the cupboard,' Stan suggested.

When the cupboard door was opened, a mouse shot out and darted across the room. The boys yelled with excitement and chased it under chairs and the sagging old sofa. It was pandemonium till it disappeared under a heavy old bookcase they could not move. Then, the chase over, they returned to the business of lighting a fire. The newspapers in the cupboard had been nibbled by the mice, but they set the wood ablaze, and the smoke belched out of the wide chimney and gave no trouble. Tin plates and mugs were taken out of haversacks, tin knives and forks laid ready. Packages of cakes and patties were added to the feast, but they had to toss a penny for the privilege of manning the frying pan.

Annie's half pound of lard was carefully rationed to fry the bread and sliced potatoes. Stan was given a slice of fried bread, blackened on one side but discreetly turned over before serving. The cook watched him anxiously, waiting for his approval.

'It tastes good. Thanks, Dennis,' he said, and smiled at the lad. Yet all the time he was conscious of that naked boy under the mackintosh, and the day was spoiled for him by its discovery.

Soon after starting the troop of Boy Scouts in the village, Stan had rejoined the church choir. It was strange, yet in a sense familiar to sit in the choir stalls where once he had helped to make local history by being one of four brothers to be singing in the choir at the same time. He remembered young Gordon, looking deceptively angelic, being specially coached by the choirmaster to sing a solo – one verse of a hymn or a passage in the anthem – on special occasions. He and his brothers had been jealous of Gordon and disgusted at all the fuss that was made of a voice they were listening to every day of the week. It was true he could soar like a bird to a top note, but so could young David Evans at choir practice. It was unfortunate for David that he suffered from stage fright and lost his nerve completely when confronted by a congregation.

The owner of the estate on which the boys had permission to camp was also a churchwarden – a privileged role afforded only to members of the upper classes. Stan had always shared his mother's respect for the gentry, so he hovered on the edge of the congregation the following Sunday morning as they filed slowly out of church.

'Excuse me, sir. Can I have a word with you?' he asked deferentially.

'Why, certainly, my good fellow. What can I do for you?'

48

'I have to make a confession, sir. I took the liberty of allowing the Scouts to shelter in the gamekeeper's cottage. It hasn't been lived in lately by the look of things, and it was raining hard. The boys were drenched but I hadn't the heart to refuse when we found the door unlocked.'

'Very sensible, Parsons. Very sensible.'

'But that's not all, sir. The boys lit a fire and used all the dry wood in the cottage. It was too wet to gather more, but we shall replace it as soon as we can get back to the woods after hop-picking. That's another six weeks, sir.'

'No need to worry, Parsons. My gamekeeper retired some years ago, so you are quite at liberty to use the cottage when the weather is bad. An artist acquaintance of mine used it for a time, but he hasn't been near the place lately. Temperamental chaps, these artists. Can't pin them down. They come and they go when the fancy takes them. We were at Cambridge together – an odd chap, but likeable.'

'The boys cleared up nicely, sir, and we left it clean and tidy.'

'Cleaner than when you found it, eh, Parsons?'

'Well, it was a little untidy, sir.'

They exchanged a meaningful glance, for artists were notoriously untidy. The congregation had dispersed and the churchwarden's wife was signalling impatiently from the doorway. Luncheon was served punctually at one o'clock, to allow Cook and the house-parlourmaid to get away at two for their free afternoon and evening. The domestics had to be considered these days. Once upon a time they were perfectly satisfied with one Sunday in the month, but not any more. Since the war they had all become so independent, demanding higher wages and shorter hours. It was quite deplorable the liberties servants were taking. Even so, friends had reminded them they were lucky to have a Cook and a house-parlourmaid when they had to make do with daily domestics from the village, or cottagers with no training at all in domestic service. Why, they couldn't even speak the King's English!

'My wife is getting impatient, Parsons. I must go,' Stan was reminded, rather brusquely, by the ex-Colonel of the Grenadier Guards. It was now or never and Stan plunged.

'I won't keep you a minute sir, but – but I found a picture of my young brother in the cottage, and now I know the artist was a friend of yours, I wondered whether you would let me have his address? You see, sir, Gordon ran away from home, and we have not been able to trace him.'

Another meaningful glance passed between them, and a moment of suspense when Stan was not sure if the request would be granted.

'The youngster with the face of a Botticelli cherub who used to sing in the choir?'

Stan had never heard of Botticelli, but he nodded agreement and hurriedly scribbled the address in his pocket book.

'If you take my advice, Parsons, you should waste no time in getting the boy back here. Good day to you!'

And he strode purposefully down the aisle.

With the start of the hop-picking season, and Annie away from the house all day, it was a good opportunity to follow the clue to London, and there Stan journeyed one September morning, clad in his best suit and boots and bowler hat. It took all his courage and determination, but this reconciliation had already been postponed too long.

By the time he reached the mews he was so nervous he could hardly speak when the door was opened and he was confronted by a bearded gentleman in corduroys and bare feet.

'Excuse me, sir, is Gordon here?' he stammered.

And when the man only gaped in astonishment, he added, 'Will you tell him it's his brother, Stan?'

'Your precious Gordon hasn't been seen here for twelve months or more. You might try Paris!' he suggested, sneeringly – and slammed the door.

Annie accepted the verdict with the same calm, stoical endurance as she had accepted Teddy's disappearance. Like father, like son. She hadn't really expected to see Gordon again. These two had used her till her usefulness had become an embarrassment, then discarded her like an outworn garment.

She kissed Stan warmly and thanked him, for she knew what it had cost his pride. Then she scrubbed her hop-stained hands and put on the kettle for a nice cup of tea.

As soon as hop-picking was over for another year, Annie, as brown as a gypsy, cleaned the house thoroughly, for it had been neglected in the six weeks of picking. When this was finished and the smell of polish pervaded every room, it was time to think about making the Christmas puddings and mincemeat. The money she had earned was put aside this year and the old tea-caddy on the mantelpiece was crammed with notes and silver. Apart from a new pair of boots, Annie intended to make do with her own clothes, since Miss Price would almost certainly provide her with a good second-hand winter coat and underwear. In return for the clothes, Annie would make her a present of a bottle of home brewed elderberry wine, hand-knitted mittens and bedsocks, for her dear friend suffered with chilblains on both hands and feet all winter.

Miss Price would join them as usual on Boxing Day for midday dinner and drive herself back to Merton Hall in the trap before dark. The groom had been one of several men of the Merton Hall staff who had not returned from the war. His lordship kept only two hunters in the stables these days, and was driven to the station in one of the new automobiles by the cook's grandson, who had escaped the war by being too young. The gentry were all obliged to accept drastic changes in their depleted households. The younger generation quickly adapted to the changed world and rather enjoyed the lack of formality, but the older generation were too conservative in their ways and reluctant to accept the new order that was thrust upon them when the war was over. The few remaining indoor servants were elderly and grey-haired; the outdoor servants greatly reduced in numbers. Two gardeners struggled to maintain the walled vegetable garden and the flower beds, but several acres of lawns had been ploughed up and planted with potatoes during the war, and were not re-turfed. Shrubberies were overgrown, empty greenhouses stank of mildew, and trees had been felled in the park. For those who had known Merton Hall in its heyday – including Miss Price, who had taken over the unenviable post of housekeeper since the war – it was sad to see the neglect.

Annie had not been back since she left the lodge when Teddy was dismissed during the first year of their marriage. It was a closed chapter, and to go back would have made her long for the old days that could never be replaced. All through the troubled years she had kept in touch with Merton Hall through Miss Price.

So Annie's 'Rainy Day Fund' in the old tea caddy was re-christened 'The Christmas Fund' that year, for every penny would be spent on making it a truly special occasion.

It would be special in so many ways, and only Gordon would be missing. There was Dick coming home with his wife expecting their first child, and, even if she would be staying with her father, she would surely visit her mother-in-law? Then she would have Tom and his wife, Ruby, spending Christmas Day with them – and that was really something to celebrate.

Looking back on that last hop-picking season, Annie would smile at the remembrance of that sudden and surprising announcement at the start of the second week of picking. Harry's resounding call 'All to work' had brought Tom hurrying back down the arches with Ben, but they were not alone. He was clasping the hand of a young woman with a grubby face and untidy hair. She was pale and thin, and her ill-fitting skirt was fastened with a large safety-pin, but Tom's face was glowing and radiant with happiness.

'Mum! This is Ruby. We are going to be married!' he shouted – and all the home-pickers looked up from their bins and smiled.

As long as she lived Annie would never forget that moment. Not in all the years of marriage and motherhood had she been more surprised.

'Married?' she echoed, her dark, searching eyes so critical of his future wife – that poor creature clinging even more tightly to Tom's hand. Then Annie realised with a sharp pang of remorse that the smudges on that pale thin face were tears that had been wiped away hurriedly with a hop-stained hand – and the young woman was scared of meeting her.

She laid down the bine that Tom had pulled before he took the dog for his daily walk and kissed her future daughter-in-law. 'That's the best news I've heard for many a long day,' she said with simple honesty. Time enough to worry about the future and sharing her home with a young Cockney from London's East End. She took Tom's glowing face in her stained hands and kissed him warmly.

'It's like a miracle, Mum, I can't believe it's actually happened. That's why I'm hanging on to her in case she slips away! You must remember Ruby, surely, Mum? We were keen on each other that last hop-picking before the war. It's a long time ago and so much has happened to both of us. Ruby has been married but she's a widow now. It makes no difference to how we feel about each other. Would you believe it, Mum, I was sitting on the bank with Ben and she was standing only a few feet away from me. "Who's there?" I said, and after a minute she answered, 'It's me – Ruby. Ruby Foster." You could have knocked me down with a feather! I still couldn't believe it. I had to feel her. Then I knew she was real and not a ghost.' He laughed and asked eagerly, 'You do remember Ruby, don't you, Mum?'

No, she wouldn't have recognised that cheeky little waif for this silent young woman clinging to Tom's hand. Why didn't she speak up for herself now that Tom had had his say? 'Yes, of course I remember Ruby,' she lied. 'She hasn't changed only to grow a few inches.'

Ruby smiled gratefully and found her tongue at last. 'Tom ain't changed neither. I would 'ave known that red 'ead a mile away.'

Annie shuddered involuntarily, but her smile was still warm and friendly. How could she possibly entertain Dick's wife and Tom's on the same day at Christmas, supposing Tom and Ruby had already married? It just wouldn't work, and she knew it wouldn't work. To enjoy the company of both she must keep them apart.

'Have I finished all the lemonade? This has given me a thirst,' Tom was saying.

'No, there's still some left in the bottle.' Annie filled the tin mug and handed it to Tom who held it out to Ruby.

'Taste it. I'll bet you've never had home-brewed lemonade eh? Mum's been making it every hop-picking since I was a little nipper.'

Ruby drank obediently, but found it insipid, and much preferred the fizzy variety from the pub. She had already decided it was better to humour Tom, and his mother was watching.

'It's nice,' she agreed, and put the mug into Tom's free hand. She knew what was wrong, for she was no fool. 'You've gotta learn me to speak proper, Tom,' she would tell him, when they were alone together.

The farmer's wife had been even more surprised than Annie when a young woman she vaguely recognised tapped on the back door of the farm house, late one evening. It had been a long day, part of it spent at the bine reserved for her in the home-set, and she was tired and ready for bed. Her 'Hello, what can I do for you?' lacked her usual cheerfulness when greeting the pickers.

'I'm Ruby Foster, Ma'am. Me an' Tom 'as just got engaged.'

'You – and – Tom?' echoed Mrs Brook. 'Hadn't you better come in and tell me about it?'

Ruby followed her into the big kitchen she had often glimpsed as a child whilst waiting to buy a penn'orth of apples at the open door. She had never expected to be invited inside.

'Sit down, Ruby, you are just in time for a cup of tea from the last brew of the day. My husband has gone over to the oast to check on the drying of a load of hops.'

They sat on either side of the hearth in comfortable wicker armchairs, and sipped the hot, strong tea, Ruby perched on the edge of the chair, leaning forward, bright-eyed and eager as a child to tell her story. She had not told Tom she would be calling at the farm, and he had gone home with his mother as usual soon after five o'clock.

'It's like this, Ma'am,' she began breathlessly. 'Me an' Tom was keen on each other before the war. I been pickin' 'ops at your farm since I was a little nipper no 'igher than the bin. Me Mum used ter bring us dahn every year. Said it was an 'oliday.' She smiled wryly.

'Well, it's a working holiday, and the clean country air must have been good for all you children from the East End,' her companion reminded her.

Ruby shook her head. 'We never felt no better for it, only we 'ad ter earn the money, see? It's all right for a week or

55

two, an' I'm not complainin', but six weeks 'opping was too long for us kids, an' we was glad ter get back 'ome. Me young sister Nellie is fed up already, an' says she's packin' it in next week an' goin' back 'ome. I can't stop 'er. She's fourteen now, an' she's got a job waitin' in a caff. She knows she can stay wiv one of our neighbours. Blimey, when I saw all them 'ops what 'as ter be picked, I was already fed up meself. Then I saw Tom was back, an' it made all the difference, see?' Her eyes widened. She shook her head again, remembering the shock of that first encounter.

'It ain't fair. Why did they 'ave ter pick on Tom, those German bastards? I couldn't make 'aht what that kid was doin' leading 'im abaht, an' that dawg what went everywhere wiv 'im. "Tom can't see. Tom's blind," they said.'

She was choked with tears for a moment, then she wiped her sleeve across her eyes and went on.

'That was a week ago an' I been tryin' ter make up me mind ter speak to 'im. Some'ow I couldn't fyce it – me seein' 'im an' 'im not seein' me. It seemed like a cheek, some'ow,' she explained, haltingly. 'It was Tom all right, but well I just 'ad ter wait an' see for a bit. It didn't tyke me long ter see the clever way 'e was managin'. Talk abaht guts! When 'e come arahnd wiv Farmer for the measurin' I couldn't tyke me eyes off 'im, Ma'am. Couldn't think of noffink but Tom all dye. Me sister Nellie says I'm a bloody wet blanket an' there ain't no fun 'avin' me at the bine. Can't blyme 'er for wantin' ter go back 'ome. She likes a bit of fun does our Nell, but it's no fun for Tom, neither, is it? What's more, I don't feel like larkin' abaht. I keep on cryin' meself ter sleep at night an' that's somethink I never done fer nobody. Tom tykes a walk wiv 'is dawg see, after 'e's ate 'is dinner, an' I been followin' 'im but not too near so 'e wouldn't know I was followin'. They sits under a n'edge, Tom an' that little dawg an' it broke me 'eart ter see Tom's fyce when 'e lifts it up as if 'e was listenin' all the time. There ain't noffink wrong wiv Tom's ears, an' 'e don't miss much. Sharp as a needle now 'e can't see. Well, there 'e sat, an' me only a few steps away. If you could 'ave seen 'is fyce, Ma'am, when I spoke to 'im an' told 'im I was Ruby Foster. It was all lit up inside. I ain't much good at explainin', but that's what it looked like ter me – all lit up inside.'

'I know what you mean, Ruby, for I've seen it for myself and it's quite wonderful. That first morning when he stood at the gate, sniffing all the farmyard smells, and again when he touched the horses he had known as a lad. But to admire Tom is natural, to want to marry him is a much graver issue, and not something to be decided on impulse. Pity is not enough. You would need the patience of a saint. Tom would drain you dry, Ruby. You haven't seen him in one of his black moods, have you? He always had a quick temper, but now it can be roused by a word spoken in haste or a misunderstanding between the person who can see and the one who can't see. Tom is stubborn as a mule, and difficult to live with. His mother and his elder brother have been so good and patient since he came home, but he rules the roost and gets his own way over everything.'

''ow d'yer know? Somebody been tellin' tales?' Ruby's voice was sharp with suspicion.

'No, not unkindly. Here in the country the postman does not only deliver the post, Ruby. We have not lost touch with Tom, even if we haven't seen him since the war. You mustn't let pity influence you, Ruby. It would not be fair to you, or to Tom.'

''oose talkin' of pity?' Ruby interrupted. 'I love Tom. I reckon I was in love wiv 'im back in 1913 only I was just a kid. I been married an' lost me 'usband in the war, but Tom knows abaht it, see, an' 'e says it don't make no difference to 'im an' me. Tom says 'e ain't never looked at another girl, an' there was only me, all them years since we said goodbye. Makes yer feel sort of proud, don't it? – an' what's more,

Tom ain't changed, neither, not fer me. I know 'e's a man, an' 'e's growed up big and strong, but Tom's still a boy at 'eart,' she insisted.

'I'm sure he is, but what will you *do* – and where will you live? If you live with his mother Tom could carry on with his basket-making, but I understand he finds it very tedious and there is no demand for them in a small village.'

'I can work. I been workin' since I was thirteen.'

'What kind of work?'

'Factory.'

'But there are no factories in a village.'

'I could do any sort o' job. I ain't afraid o' work, Ma'am.'

The silence between them was pregnant with Ruby's unasked question, and the farmer's wife sighed before she answered. 'You mean you would be willing to leave London and live in the country?'

Ruby nodded vigorously, but her worried companion still hesitated.

'I could use another pair of hands, Ruby, for we lost Mary-Ann in the 'flu epidemic and I have not been able to replace her.'

'A servant?'

'Yes, a servant.'

It was Ruby's turn to hesitate. 'I ain't never been in service. Us Cockneys don't tyke to service, seems like servants is jus' slaves?'

'Not any more, Ruby, not since the war. And anyway, our servants have always been regarded as trusted and loyal friends. I would not expect you to do anything I was not prepared to do myself, and there is no uniform, other than a white apron, similar to the one I am wearing. We are not gentry, Ruby. We are working farmers, but I'm warning you, it's a hard life for a woman and doesn't compare with a factory. The work on a farm is never finished, indoors or out. You must be willing to help the other wives in the hop-

58

gardens at stringing time, as well as fruit picking and hop-picking. We all pull together in a farming community and nobody expects any free time at haymaking, harvest and hop-picking. Do you understand what it means, Ruby? Should you not think it over before committing yourself.'

'I been thinkin' it over all dye – since I asked Tom ter marry me.'

'*You* asked *Tom*? Oh, Ruby!' Mrs Brook chuckled happily. 'I believe you and I will get along fine. As for Tom, he's a lucky fellow. Well, we have settled your immediate problem, but we still have to reckon with Tom. Shall we leave it to the men to settle between them? I know my husband could use another pair of hands, outdoors. Perhaps Tom could help Harry? He's a kind soul with the patience of Job. By the way, there's an empty cottage. Leave it to me. I'll speak to my husband.'

'Coo, *Ma'am*!' Ruby exclaimed, as she went out. 'You ain't arf a one!'

'Where's your wife?' asked Annie, anxiously that Christmas Eve, when she opened the door to find Dick on the threshold.

'She was tired, Mother, and asked to be excused. She sent her kind regards.'

'Come in, son,' she said, quietly. A daughter-in-law who sent her kind regards? What sort of a woman was this wife of Dick's that she couldn't bring herself to set foot in her husband's home? Annie was both relieved and annoyed, for she had worked so hard to have the place clean and shining for this first visit. She knew, of course, that her son's wife would be staying in her old home, but nothing further had been mentioned in Dick's recent letter. He hadn't even told them the time of arrival, or Stan would have met the train.

'There's a one-man taxi service from the station now, so

we dropped Linda off in the village and I stayed a minute or two to greet her father. The old nurse was delighted to have Linda back, and made a great fuss of her.'

Annie kissed him warmly, took his coat and hat and asked, 'How long can you stay?'

'Three days.'

'Only three days?' Annie's face clouded with disappointment, for she had expected him to stay for at least a week.

'Linda wanted to spend the rest of the Christmas holiday in Switzerland. She knows Switzerland very well. The whole family would go to Davos for the winter sports before the war.'

'But the baby? She can't? – She won't. . . .'

'No. Only watching this year. I'm afraid she is going to be bored. But the holiday will do her good for she hasn't been at all well – nerves, mostly. Linda is very highly strung.'

'She is pleased about the baby?'

Dick shook his head sadly. 'Every woman is not a born mother like you. It's too soon. She had no time for fun after slogging away in hospital during the war.'

'Fun? What sort of fun was she expecting?'

'Oh, the usual – parties and dances, an occasional show in London, that sort of thing, but she just hasn't felt like making the effort even to see a show. I've been very worried about her, that's why I encouraged this Swiss holiday. Switzerland is renowned for its healthy climate, and there are sanatoriums for tubercular patients up in the mountains – for those who can afford it,' he added truthfully.

Annie was looking at her son with a mother's discerning eyes. His wife was not the only one who would benefit from this holiday, she thought. Dick was pale and thin and there was a strained look in his serious grey eyes. But he was married to this highly-strung young woman who wanted to have fun and found herself pregnant. She knew Dick's loyalty would not allow a word of reproach so she merely agreed the holiday was a good idea, pushed him gently on to the sagging sofa and waited for the kettle to boil. While she brewed the tea, he held his thin, blue-veined hands to the blazing fire and looked about him with pleasure in the old home where nothing seemed to change.

When Stan came in from the workshop to join them in a cup of tea, Dick sprang to his feet to shake hands with his brother. Such nice polite manners, his mother was thinking, as she listened to Dick explaining all over again about his wife's tiredness, her regards, and the reason why his visit would be restricted to only three days. Stan was sensible enough to make no comment, but when Dick had taken a little walk to the privy, he agreed with his mother that all was not right with this marriage. A good many of these hurried wartime marriages would break up, Stan contended. Why hadn't Dick waited till the war was over and he was feeling fit – not that the poor blighter would ever be really fit with that mustard gas in his lungs.

'I don't think it has anything to do with Dick's health. It's like I said in the beginning, Stan, it's a mistake to marry out of your own class. Dick's had that extra bit of education and he looks like a gentleman and behaves like a gentleman, but it doesn't alter the fact we are working-class, and his own mother was a washerwoman at one time. He won't say a word against her, but I have a very strong feeling they had a few words when she asked to be dropped in the village. After all, it was only a short distance, and she could have shown herself, even for a few minutes. It wasn't kind to Dick,' Annie protested, for she could speak her mind to her eldest son.

'Well, if she's such a bloody snob she can stop away!' he retorted vehemently.

'Hush, Stan. Dick might hear you. It is Christmas and I won't have any upset.'

61

'All right, Mum, I'll be careful. Anyway, we shall have Tom and Ruby tomorrow, and we shan't have to mind our p's and q's with those two. I like that little Cockney wife of Tom's. She's genuine, and she's darn plucky. Not many girls would have taken on such a responsibility, but then, she's obviously in love with him and that makes a difference.'

'And Tom worships the ground she walks on,' Annie reminded him. 'I wouldn't be surprised to hear there was a baby on the way already, for they both want a big family.'

'I see Tom's little workshop is empty,' said Dick, coming back into the room. 'It was a good idea of yours, Stan, but I guess Tom wanted something more active than basket-making. I was sorry I couldn't get down for the wedding, but it's difficult to get away during the term. It was a chapel wedding, wasn't it? Any particular reason for chapel instead of church?'

'It was more convenient for everyone. All the farm people go to chapel and it's only about a mile or so from the farm,' Annie explained. 'The farmer and his wife have been wonderful. They paid for the wedding and had the wedding breakfast in the big farm kitchen. We enjoyed it, didn't we Stan?'

'Every minute,' he agreed. 'It's taken a load off our minds, Dick, I don't mind telling you. It hasn't been easy to keep the peace since Tom came home for good. Poor devil. Some days he didn't know where to put himself he was so restless and frustrated.'

Dick listened to his brother with a sense of shame that he hadn't shared the burden, or even spent a few days at home from time to time. There was no excuse, and he should have made an effort. Now it was too late. Tom was back where he rightly belonged, among country people, who understood his mentality. Tomorrow he would meet his younger brother and this staunch young woman he had married. It would be strange to feel envious of this couple, who seemed to have started married life with all the odds against them, and yet had already found happiness and contentment – according to Stan and his mother.

The last delivery of mail early Christmas morning brought a gaudy greetings card with a foreign stamp.

'It's from Gordon! Stan! Dick! A Christmas card from Gordon!' cried Annie excitedly. Then, remembering the traditional hospitality, invited the postman to step inside for a glass of elderberry wine and a mince-pie. They crowded round her while Dick translated the simple verse and listened in wonder to his cleverness. It was nothing to boast about and any one of his young pupils could have managed it equally well, but it boosted Dick's morale to be so admired and appreciated, for he had been suffering badly from an inferiority complex of late, in the cultured company of his wife and her cousin Roger. The card was signed in a sprawling childish hand *Love to all, Gordon*. There was no address, so he obviously had no wish to receive letters from his family.

'That artist chap was right. He said to try Paris,' Stan reflected, while his mother arranged the precious tribute on the mantelpiece, already crowded with Christmas cards.

'It's made my day,' she told them, starry-eyed as a young sweetheart who had received an unexpected greeting from an absent lover.

The postman went on his way with his heavy load of mail, but nothing he delivered that morning would bring more pleasure than Annie's card. 'Annie Parsons has heard from her youngest son and he's living in Paris,' he would tell the neighbours, and they would marvel at this further evidence that Annie's Boys were doing well for themselves.

Stan and Dick, wearing their best suits, hovered around

their mother all morning, sniffing the succulent juices of roast beef. The Christmas pudding was getting its final boiling in the big iron pot. Stan had been out in the garden early to pick the brussels sprouts and had peeled potatoes for roasting. It was Stan who had draped the beams with home-made paper chains and tramped across the fields in search of evergreens to hang over the pictures. Nobody ever expected Dick to help with such mundane tasks and it did not occur to him to offer!

Annie's face was flushed from the heat of the stove and the excitement. Three of her boys would be home for Christmas Day, and the fourth had sent a card to set her mind at rest that he was still alive and well. The firelight danced on the old oak beams, the shining fender and the polished brass. Freshly starched antimacassars draped the chairs and sofa, but would soon be crumpled when Tom's restless head made contact with them.

Dick went to stand at the front gate at midday to welcome his younger brother and the wife he had not yet met. Then he saw them stepping briskly down the road. So they had walked the two miles from the farm, and would walk back tonight. Dick's throat tightened and tears pricked his eyes, yet there was nothing pathetic in that little group. Tom had the dog on a leash and was clasping the hand of his young wife who carried a bulging bag of presents and a bunch of holly. They both were dressed up in their wedding outfits, and Tom's bowler hat sat incongruously on his red head. Ruby was so proud of her new clothes – the first time in her life she had actually bought clothes in a shop. She and Tom had spent a day in Tunbridge Wells together and spent all the money they had earned during the six weeks of hop-picking. If she appeared to Dick a little overdressed, and the hat too large for her small, peaked face, he gave no sign of it, but smiled a welcome. Now she was telling Tom that his brother was waiting at the gate, and Tom's lifted, listening face was beaming.

'Hello, Dick!' he called out.

'Hello, Tom!'

The brothers clasped hands over the gate, then Tom's arm slid protectively about his wife's shoulders, for he knew she was shy of meeting Dick. Stan was different, and they were already good friends. It was not her first visit to Tom's home, and she had lost her shyness of his mother. Now she regarded this tall, distinguished-looking stranger in the well-cut suit and school tie, and was tongue-tied. Tom didn't want her to change. He loved the little Cockney he had married, but Ruby was still determined to 'speak proper'.

''ullo – 'appy Christmas,' was all she could say at that moment of meeting.

'Happy Christmas, Ruby,' said Dick, feelingly – and kissed her cheek.

The door stood invitingly open, and the welcome was warm and homely. In the cheerful company of the three brothers, Ruby quickly forgot her shyness, and lapsed into a mixture of Cockney and countrified Kent dialect that was really funny. But Tom's voice was the loudest and Tom's laugh the most merry of the three brothers. He had to be noticed and applauded all the time, like a spoilt child. He drank too much elderberry wine, had two helpings of beef and Christmas pudding, stuffed himself with nuts, dates, muscatels and raisins, chocolates and marshmallows all afternoon, and was still ready for tea at five o'clock. Ruby plied him with bread and butter spread with strawberry jam, sweet biscuits and rich plum cake, while Annie re-filled his tea cup four times. Stan and Dick marvelled at such an insatiable appetite for food and drink. Ruby was as proud and pleased with Tom as a hen with one chick, but, for all his boasting and self-assurance, they noticed that his hand searched for hers as soon as he finished the meal.

To please Annie they gathered round the piano in the late evening to sing carols, Tom's red head was aflame in the candlelight, his voice strong. He remembered every word of every carol from his boyhood in the choir, and so did Stan. Dick could accompany them providing he had the music for he hadn't his father's natural talent, or his light touch. Annie leaned back comfortably in the armchair, closed her eyes and thought of Teddy. Christmas was a time to remember those who once had shared the festive season. She wondered if he was enjoying his Christmas in South Africa, and if he was still living with that wealthy widow he had bigamously married. Her mouth trembled on a smile. There was no bitterness, no reproach, and never had been. She knew her Teddy – her restless, unreliable, unpredictable Teddy!

Ruby was singing *Away in a Manger*, and now Teddy was forgotten. Annie was back at the Girls' Home in a long pinafore and button boots. She began to sing softly, her face in the firelight was pale now, her dark eyes shadowed. It was nearly midnight and it had been a long, exciting day.

'There's a baby on the way, Mum,' Ruby whispered as she hugged her mother-in-law and thanked her for a lovely day.

'Well, that's really crowned my Christmas Day!' said Annie, joyfully.

'*Two* grandchildren, Mother, before another Christmas,' Dick reminded her quickly.

Stan was lighting the cycle lamp that Ruby would carry to light their way down the dark country roads. With Tom clasping her hand and Ben as watchdog, she would still feel nervous. In fact, she would never conquer her fear of the darkness that surrounded them beyond the walls of their cottage, or these winter nights. It was terrifying to her city-bred eyes to be confronted by this awful blackness and she

66

would hurry to the privy in shivering terror, with the lantern. Yet Tom lived in perpetual darkness now. How could he bear it? She would go mad. Some days he was so beaten and frustrated he would cry with rage, and she would rock him in her arms, his wet face at her breast, soothing him till he was quiet. She never told anyone, and only Ruby saw Tom's tears or grappled with his violent temper. The farmer's wife had been right to warn her, for living with Tom could be both heaven and hell. Yet she managed him in her own way, and lost none of her individuality.

'The stink of carbide brings back memories, doesn't it, Stan?' Tom was saying, as they waited for the cycle lamp. 'Remember that first bike you put together, and you and me got halfway to Tunbridge Wells when the bloody lamp went out!'

'I never knew whether it would be Stan or Tom brought home with a broken limb or a bleeding head, but it was usually Tom,' his mother explained, and there was pride in her voice, though once upon a time she had wished he could be a little less reckless and daring. Oh, but she was proud of him now, and she must tell him so, for so often she had missed an opportunity in her natural reticence, her dislike of making a fuss. Ruby had shown her, indeed had shamed her. Tom had to be loved by touch, by the tone of a voice, by constant reassurance. Her little Cockney daughter-in-law had succeeded where she and Stan had failed.

When she took Tom's face in her hands and kissed him so warmly, he was surprised to discover she was crying.

'What's up, Mum? Something upset you?' he demanded.

'No, my boy. Nothing could upset me today. Didn't you know a woman always cries when she's most happy? And I'm going to be a grandmother before another Christmas, as if that wasn't a good enough reason to have a good cry!'

They laughed at her then, and teased her, but it was Dick who slipped an arm about her waist at the garden gate, and it was Dick's handkerchief she found in her hand as the darting ray of light pierced the darkness of the night and two young voices called back their final, 'Goodnight, Mum!'

'A last cup of tea, eh, Mum?'

Stan pushed the kettle over the fire and stooped to stroke the cat on the hearth.

'They're just right for each other, those two,' he said, meaningly – and Dick agreed.

Chapter Three

During the next five years Annie was rewarded with five grandchildren, and the family circle widened on Christmas Day with a new generation of children to be loved and spoiled by a doting Granny. It was disappointing to see so little of her first grandchild, but there seemed to be nothing she could do to change a situation in which Dick's wife always had the last word. Just a glimpse of the child once a year, on Christmas Eve, and a few brief moments of exquisite joy when she held the child in her arms. Then she was gone, with the old nurse who took charge of her from the moment she arrived.

'We have a little girl, Mother, and she is like you. We have called her Lucy and we hope you will like the name,' Dick had written.

When Annie saw the baby that first Christmas she seemed to be looking at a reflection of herself in miniature.

'Such a quaint little soul,' she murmured, her eyes tender with love for Dick's child. It was not a happy marriage, but her son would not speak of the differences and dissensions that divided them. Once the baby had been taken away by the nurse, he settled down quietly in the old home, as though he had never been away, but he was obviously reluctant to talk about his life at the school, so they did not press him. In three days he would be gone to join his wife and her cousin for the winter sports holiday at Davos – sports too strenuous for Dick but much enjoyed by Linda and Roger. The baby was left behind with the nurse and

Annie did not see the child again.

'But I could look after her, Dick, while you are away?' she pleaded eagerly that first Christmas.

'None better, Mother, don't I know it, but Linda wants it this way,' he said.

She did not argue with him or remind him he had equal rights to decide what was best for the child, for she knew it was only by appeasing his wife and not opposing her that their life together could be bearable.

'Then I shall never get to know my first grandchild,' Annie told Stan sadly, for Dick and Linda spent all the Summer vacation in Italy and took a young nursemaid to look after the baby.

'It's a shame, Mum, but I can't see that you can do anything about it at the moment. Wait and see what happens. The marriage could break up.'

'I hope it won't for the child's sake. Every child needs two parents. You boys were deprived of a father when you were little for he was always away.'

'I shouldn't worry any more on that old score, Mum, for we didn't notice we were being deprived. In fact, I seem to remember the trouble started when Dad did come home!'

Annie sighed. 'There are some things in this life we just have to put up with whether we like it or not, for you can't change human nature. Perhaps I'm too soft, too easy-going. Folks said I spoiled you boys because you were never punished, but I saw too much of it at the Girls' Home. Mind you, there were times when I was so provoked I could easily have laid about me with the carpet beater! Not you, Stan, or Dick. You were good boys, but Tom and Gordon often tried my patience.'

'You were the best Mum in the world, and you still are, for that matter,' Stan declared stoutly.

'I did my best,' was all she said.

Now it was Dick's child she worried about, and little

Lucy whose future was at stake. This was something that only a husband and wife could decide for themselves. Stan was right. She must wait and see and not interfere.

'You've got other grandchildren,' he reminded her kindly. 'Ruby seems to have no difficulty in producing a baby every year, and Tom dotes on them, but I'm wondering how many more they can squeeze into that small cottage.'

'The last one is a boy. That makes two of each so perhaps they will be satisfied now. It's a nice little family,' his mother suggested.

She often had the whole family for the day on Sunday for she preferred to entertain them in her own home. Ruby's methods of housekeeping and bringing up a family were completely alien to her own, but Tom was happy and the children were healthy enough, so Annie kept her thoughts to herself, and managed to change smelly nappies, wipe noses and mop up dribbling chins without upsetting Ruby!

The hop-picking season brought them together every working day for six weeks, since Ruby brought her babies to the hop-garden in the iron-wheeled pramcart that once had carried Annie's babies. The two women shared a bin divided into two halves, but it was Annie who comforted a crying child, or nursed little Maudie on her knees at the bine when she was tired of playing in the dirt.

The eldest girl, Rosie, at the age of four was already capable of leading her father by the hand to pull the bines for the home-pickers and to stand beside him while the hops were measured into the sacks. The children accepted a blinded father as naturally as they accepted their mother's cuffs. Little Sammy would be lifted on to Duke's broad back while the wagon was loaded, and Tom would take the baby in his arms and cuddle him after his midday feed and laugh at its wet bottom and dribbling chin. The elder children soon learned to keep out of his way when Tom's

71

temper flared as suddenly as the coals in the stove, for he quickly made amends, and children are adaptable creatures. It was fun to be carried on his shoulders down the long green archways, reaching up to pick hops, with Ben leading the way and their young mother close at their heels with the baby tucked under her arm like an untidy parcel!

They were poor, but Ruby had never known anything but poverty and seemed to thrive on hardship. Annie had emptied her cupboard of baby clothes, keeping only the nappies and the bibs, for she was horrified to find her grandchildren with bare bottoms! She had given them the pram and the cradle when Rosie was born, and now she would start to cut up old skirts for frocks and knickers. When the children started school they must look respectable, or the teachers would think they were gypsies! Ruby Parsons was doing her best, as all the neighbours agreed, and no woman could work harder, what with helping at the farmhouse and all the field work in season. Tom was strong and willing, but his capacity was naturally limited. It was Ruby who carried the burden of his blindness and comforted him when he was defeated by a job he had tackled so bravely. Sometimes she wondered why she had chosen such an alien way of life and when her Cockney friends waved goodbye from the piled wagons, she wanted to climb up and join them.

But Tom's arm was heavy about her shoulders. Tom understood and he knew she would cry after they had gone. Tom loved her and needed her. Every woman likes to be loved and needed by someone.

When the taxi stopped at the house and Dick lifted out his small daughter, Annie was not unduly surprised, for she had been half expecting it for some time. She hurried out eagerly to open the gate and smile a welcome. The solemn little girl stared back at her, wide-eyed, clutching her

72

father with one hand, hugging a doll and a Teddy Bear with the other. The driver carried in the luggage, then she walked beside her father down the garden path, and entered the house that would be her home until she was married. Dick was quiet and calm as usual, and the child was trusting and obedient.

When the driver had been paid and received a generous tip, Dick kissed his mother warmly and she whispered, 'You're staying?'

He nodded, and they both looked down at the child with a single thought – 'How could any mother bear to part with her?'

With her small piquant face, dark eyes, and long shining brown hair, she was a very appealing little girl. But who had sent the child away so immaculately dressed, Annie wondered? The tailored coat and matching poke-bonnet, the buttoned leather leggings, could be seen on any little girl taking a walk with her nurse in Hyde Park, or riding to church in the family carriage from some big estate in the country. Somebody had fastened all those buttons on her leggings, somebody had washed and brushed that shining hair, somebody had dressed the doll and the Teddy Bear in hand-knitted woollies.

'Give Granny a nice kiss, sweetheart,' said Dick coaxingly, and Lucy obediently held up her face.

'I want Jenny,' she said decisively. Who was Jenny? Annie wondered.

'Jenny is having a holiday with *her* Granny while you have a holiday with *your* Granny. Do you remember, pet, I explained about the holidays?'

Lucy nodded and seemed quite satisfied. Annie checked the impulse to fold the child in her arms. She must wait. She was a stranger to the little girl. Now the bright eyes were travelling about the room – glancing up at the paper chains Stan had strung across the beams. A bright fire

73

blazed in the shining stove and a cat was curled on the hearthrug. A small Christmas tree stood on top of the piano, draped in tinsel and silver bells. The table was spread with afternoon tea on a white cloth. It was warm and cosy after the long, cold journey.

'It's nice,' said the child, and laid her cherished companions on the sofa. 'Take off my coat and hat, Daddy,' she ordered with the air of one accustomed to prompt service. So Jenny was the nursemaid? Dick smiled and obeyed. Annie watched her son fumbling with the buttons on the leggings, but did not offer to help. It was strange to see her clever son in the role of a father. They obviously adored one another.

'Daddy – *my* Daddy,' Lucy told Annie, and stroked his cheek.

'Hullo, Dick! Hello, Lucy! Happy Christmas!' said Stan in the doorway. He too waited for the child to take her own time. There was no hurry, not this Christmas. Judging by the luggage they had come to stay.

But Stan had only to look at the child to know he would be her slave. 'Just starting to snow. It's going to be a white Christmas!' he told them gleefully.

When it was time for bed, and Annie stood hesitating, looking down at the tired little girl on her father's lap, Stan said quietly, 'I'll sleep on the sofa, Mum.' Dick was troubled by the arrangement, but could see no alternative, so he undressed Lucy and carried her upstairs. Annie had wrapped a hot brick in a piece of flannel to warm the bed.

Stan was enchanted with his little niece in her pink flannelette nightgown, her eyes drooping with sleep.

'Say goodnight to Uncle Stan,' his brother said, and when the child's soft mouth brushed his lips he was reminded of Kathie in those early years before the war. The doors were left open, the doll and the Teddy Bear tucked in beside her, and a nightlight left burning on the chest of drawers.

Annie was busy on the final preparations for Christmas Day, and when she had filled a pillow case with presents for Lucy, she left the brothers together.

'You don't mind if we stay here, Mother?' Dick asked quietly later.

'How can you ask such a question, son? This is your home.'

'Thank you.'

'You see, Linda wants to marry her cousin Roger.'

Annie made no reply and neither did Stan. But what will Dick do now, Stan was wondering. He had a good job at the school, and was not strong enough for manual work. Annie's thoughts were free of anxiety as she hung the bulging pillow case at the foot of Lucy's bed. Such unexpected joy this Christmas Eve left no room for doubt and sorrow. Last year the child was too young to remember, but at four years old a child has left babyhood behind.

Stan need not have worried about the future, for Dick had been making plans for some months, and this was no hasty decision.

'I've been offered a teaching post at the village school,' he told his mother, as he perched on her bed early the next morning, watching Lucy unwrap her presents. 'I wrote to ask for the next vacancy, and was offered the post immediately on the strength of Roger's recommendation. He has been very fair, I must say. After all, he engaged me in the first place without any teaching qualifications. I start the first week of January.'

Their eyes met and held over the child's innocent head.

'I'm glad,' said Annie simply.

Three days later Lucy announced that she would sleep with Granny in the big bed. 'It's a nice, comfy bed, and Granny is a nice, comfy Granny.'

In her newfound happiness and contentment, however, Annie was soon reminded of that other grandparent and the possessive old nurse only a short distance away. Lucy had to spend Boxing Day at her mother's old home, and would be expected for tea every Sunday.

When Dick collected his small daughter in the evening of that first Boxing Day, he was obliged to push a big expensive doll's pram in which two dolls were seated, elaborately dressed in silk and satin, with buckled shoes and Edwardian hats. There was a parcel, also, containing a red velvet party frock and a new red dressing-gown and slippers. Dick found it embarrassing to return home with such expensive presents, for the gifts from his own family had been bought at the village Christmas Bazaar, and Stan had made the small cradle for the tiny baby doll that Annie had dressed in a flannel nightgown.

'Look what Grandpa and Nanny have given me,' said Lucy, proudly. 'And I was allowed to choose the pudding for lunch – and I wore a serviette round my neck, not a bib – and Grandpa let me play with his steth – steth –?'

'Stethoscope,' said Dick with a tolerant smile.

She was tired and tiresome after all the spoiling, and started to cry when she was being undressed. It was a pity, Dick thought, that they had to live in the same village as his wife's relations, but it was the two old favourites in their woollies that Lucy wanted in her bed, and Stan's cradle with the tiny doll stood on the chair beside the bed. It was all the little things she played with, they noticed, and the big expensive pram with the elaborately dressed dolls was proudly displayed on the Sunday afternoon walks, then forgotten for the rest of the week.

Stan was making a doll's house, and every evening when the tea had been cleared, it was assembled on the table. Lucy stood watching, leaning on her elbows, completely absorbed, while Dick checked compositions in grubby

76

exercise books, and marked them carefully with a blue and a red pencil.

'That Lucy knows all 'er letters and can write 'er own name, and she only four,' Ruby told Tom.

'And so she should with a schoolteacher for a father. Our Rosie can feed the hens and collect the eggs. She's my eyes, she takes me wherever I want to go and tells what she sees. There are different kinds of cleverness, Luv, and our kids are all as bright as buttons. So don't you fret about book learning and schooling. Dick's Lucy is too quiet for me, it's not natural for a child to be so good and obedient. I bet Mum likes to have our kids around the place on Sunday, the noisy little devils!'

It was more a question of putting up with it than liking it, as Annie confessed to her two quiet sons as they cleared up the debris, swept up the crumbs and wiped sticky chairs after the family had left. Then she would hurry off to church as the five-minute bell was tolling, and be thankful it was Dick and not Tom who had sought refuge under her roof.

'Wait for me, Granny.'

'Leave the door open, Granny.'

That dark little privy in the garden was a place to avoid, even at the risk of wet knickers, but Annie discovered she had unlimited time and patience for this small grand-daughter. It was not to be compared with those early years, when four growing boys and the washing had kept her busy from early morning till late evening. If she was spoiling the child with too much attention, she was a willing slave and had the excuse Lucy had no mother and was accustomed to a devoted nursemaid. It was such a joy to see little garments airing on the fireguard, to have a child's demanding voice calling, 'Granny! I want you, Granny'. The eternal questions she often had to leave for Dick to answer, the

77

offers of help that were such a hindrance. Her little world was a pleasant place again, now that it was blessed with a child. They were constant companions that first spring and summer, and the contentment was reflected from the woman to the child, as their days followed the same quiet pattern till one morning in late summer, when they set off together to the farm. Lucy was riding in a push-chair, nursing her two old favourites.

At the age of four Annie's boys had been expected to walk everywhere, but not Lucy. The push-cart was hung with all the paraphernalia necessary to a day in the hop-garden. But Lucy did not share her grandmother's pleasure in this seasonal event. The swarming new world of Cockneys, gypsies and home-pickers confused and frightened her. Neither did she mix very well with the four young cousins in their home environment.

'She's too genteel, that Lucy,' Ruby complained, comparing Tom's tow-headed little urchins with Dick's demure little girl. There was an *Alice in Wonderland* look about her, with her long straight hair, fastened by a band of ribboned elastic, her starched white pinafore and brown button boots. The button boots were considered old-fashioned now, and home-pickers' children wore rubber Wellingtons, including her cousins, Rosie and Maudie.

When the sun shone hot through the clearing where the bines had been pulled, Annie would tie a sunbonnet on Lucy's head. With Ruby and Tom picking hops in the adjoining bine, all five children shared the sweets and cakes that Annie always carried in her bag, and Lucy was obliged to watch a small cousin being nursed in the dinner hour on a lap she considered her own special property.

There would be no compulsion as the years went by, although Lucy could not escape the annual migration to the hop-gardens. She would pick the hops only when she was so disposed, in cotton gloves! For the rest of the day she

78

would be free to wander along the hedgerows gathering wild flowers, or furtively watching other children. She was curious about other children, and fascinated by the black-eyed, barefoot gypsies, but too shy and scared to make contact.

'Can we go home now, Granny?' The constant question amused Tom and Ruby.

'Not yet, dear,' Annie would answer patiently. On the stroke of five Harry's resonant voice would echo across the garden – 'No more bines to be pulled today!' And Lucy would run back, her face bright with eagerness.

'Now, can we go home, Granny?'

Dick would be waiting at the gate, Stan would have the tea laid and the kettle boiling.

'I don't like hop-picking, Daddy,' said Lucy, decidedly, that first day.

He scooped her up in his arms. 'Why not? Why don't you like it, Sweetheart?'

Lucy shook her head. How could she explain that she wanted to stay in this safe, familiar little world, with the three people she loved best.

'I expect you will like it better when you get used to it,' Dick suggested.

'No, I won't ever like hop-picking, Daddy,' she insisted.

'Well, neither did I, so that makes two of us!' he laughed.

On that first morning of Lucy's schooldays, she had been too excited to eat her breakfast, and went off with Dick, holding his hand, a small leather satchel on her back. Annie waved from the gate till they were out of sight.

Lucy was very conscious of her importance as the daughter of the only male teacher. So few young men had been spared to return to the teaching profession after the war. All the children they met on the way acknowledged him politely, the boys touching their caps as they had been taught by respectful parents. Although the girls no longer curtsied, as in their mother's day, they smiled shyly. 'Good morning, sir!' followed them down the village street, and all the children turned to stare at the small girl in a tailored cost and matching poke bonnet. Lucy was wearing her second-best, the best being kept for Sundays and visits to Grandfather. Dr Pearce had retired, but still lived in the house where her own mother had spent her childhood. He was looking out for them and waved from a window as they went by. Already that mother figure was growing a little dim in Lucy's memory, for she had not played a very important part in her early life, and Lucy had been a little afraid of her. It was Jenny, the young nursemaid, she recalled so vividly, for they had been together as far back as she could remember, until they came to live with Granny.

Of all the people in her small world she loved her father best. She had enjoyed that safe, comfortable little world for a whole year now, and the rough and tumble of the village school was a shock for which she was not prepared. Sheltered and cosseted like a little bird in a nest, it was time now to spread her wings. Under her father's protection, she had no fear, no anticipation of the dangers that awaited her when he was no longer there. He had told her about the infants classroom, with its tiny tables and chairs, the slates and the coloured chalks, the copy books and picture books, and she was eager to see it for herself. In her new satchel she carried a new pencil box, containing not only pencils but a rubber and a sharpener, even a ruler. It was a present from Uncle Stan on her fifth birthday, and he had explained about the measurements on the ruler. The pen-holder and the nibs she would not be allowed to use in the Infants, because ink was too messy. She knew so much about so many things, for the three loving people in her small world of home were never too busy or too tired to explain or to answer her questions. She knew her alphabet, could write her name and address, read a simple little story with short words, and count up to a hundred. It was her father, of course, who taught her to read and write and count. From Uncle Stan she had learned how to pump up a tyre, oil the pedals, and polish the spokes. He had given her a tiny puncture outfit and an old tyre to practise on. Once upon a time there had been a girl called Kathie, who used to sit quietly on the chair and watch the work, nursing a cat on her lap. She knew all about Kathie, but although she reminded Uncle Stan of this other girl, Lucy knew she was not really like her, and didn't want to be. She wanted to be herself.

From Granny she had learned how to make a bed. She loved the smell of the lavender-bags tucked in the pillows, and the smell of clean sheets that had blown on the line in the garden. She had her own special duster to dust the chairs and the piano. When she was seven, she would be having lessons, and would play the piano like Grandfather Parsons, who used to play very well at one time, so Granny said. She knew how to make gingerbread – well, almost – and all the odd pieces of pastry were turned into little men, with raisins for eyes and raisins to fasten their jackets. There was a time for picking currants and gooseberries, a time for digging potatoes, a time for radishes and a time for brussels sprouts; even a time when there was nothing in the garden but cabbage stalks. They had done everything together for a whole year, but now she had left Granny behind. In her excitement and eagerness to get to school, she had actually forgotten to kiss her goodbye and had to be reminded. The safe little world she had left behind seemed very far away as she entered the school gate, walked across the empty playground and into the sudden bedlam of the crowded, noisy cloakroom. Big girls were fighting each other, and little girls with dirty noses and dirty pinafores were chasing each other round the rows of hanging coats.

A sudden silence fell on the cloakroom when Dick

81

Parsons entered with his small daughter, then Tom's two children ran out from behind the group of staring girls to greet their cousin. It was no surprise to Rosie and Maudie to see Lucy dressed so smartly, for even in the hop-garden, in her third-best clothes, she always looked and behaved like a little lady. But they were surprised to see her standing there, waiting to be undressed, and so were the other children surprised. In big families the older children helped the younger ones. For all her cleverness, Lucy was not yet expected to dress and undress herself. It was Annie's fault and Annie's mistake to cling too long to the habits of early years.

'Lucy Parsons is a baby,' these critical eyes were saying, as they watched the father unbutton her coat and take off her bonnet.

'Hullo, Lucy!' piped her cousins excitedly, but Lucy was speechless with shock and dismay.

'We got new pinnies, see?' Maudie was saying. 'Our Mum made 'em,' she added, proudly.

They were coloured pinafores, and obviously hand-made, for Ruby was a poor needlewoman. She had cut up a faded cotton dress, as proof of her independence rather than be beholden to Tom's mother for everything.

'You having your dinner at school then?' Rosie demanded, and Dick answered, 'yes' – smiling down at their shining, eager faces. He had never seen Tom's children looking so clean.

'We got our dinner, me and Maudie. Our Mum says we can have a fry-up for tea. You know, bubble and squeak.'

'Very nice,' said Dick. Children were alike in one respect, he thought. It was always Mum who was the central figure in their world, as it had been in his own boyhood.

Lucy's dark eyes were pleading, and he wished now he had warned her against this sudden alarming impact of a

82

crowd of staring, unfriendly faces. She was too sensitive, too vulnerable for this type of school. Why hadn't he accepted the generous offer from his father-in-law to pay the fees of a private school? His own pride had not allowed him to accept anything more than the expensive clothes and toys it was so difficult to refuse. So he had mollified the old man with a promise of Grammar School later, if Lucy passed her examinations.

'It will be all right, sweetheart,' he told her, gently, his heart torn with love and pity. Then he took her hand and led the way to the Infants' classroom, followed by Rosie and Maudie, as cheekily self-assured as their Cockney mother.

Chapter Four

'What's the matter with Sammy?' Tom demanded gruffly, as he listened to the scolding and scuffling in the adjoining bedroom where three of the children slept.

'He keeps falling abaht, says his legs hurt. Growing pains, I reckon.'

Ruby had worked hard in her first year of marriage to copy Tom, who 'talked proper', but the Cockney idiom would never be entirely eliminated, neither did Tom wish it. Her courage and cheerfulness was the mainstay of his small world. Tom's temper was short, and her own limited patience often exhausted, so the children suffered. It was natural that he should demand more than his share of attention, and she did her best, but even her best was not enough some days, when she had to choose between her husband and her children, because she could not tear herself apart. Then it was Tom who claimed her, and the children who were neglected. On his 'bad' days – and all handicapped people have their bad days – he was so depressed and frustrated he was like a bear with a sore head, and she was thankful to get to bed. Here, in the gloomy darkness that frightened her, after the lighted streets of London, she was aware that Tom endured perpetual darkness, so she was never too tired to satisfy his strong, demanding body.

Tom's virility was increased, not impaired by his blindness. He knew no inhibitions in the marriage bed. The sense of touch fully compensated for that missing sense of sight. It was no longer necessary to see Ruby when he knew her so intimately by touch. She was still small and skinny, and she came to bed unwashed, but no other woman could have given him so much sensual pleasure and satisfaction.

If the baby cried in the cradle beside the marriage bed, Ruby would step out, put a dummy in its mouth, and be back in Tom's arms before he had time to miss her. They had their favourites. Rosie, the eldest girl, was Tom's favourite. Sammy, the eldest boy, was Ruby's. It may have been the reason for Maudie's naughtiness, for children are always aware of this distinction at an early age. Tom's face would brighten at the sound of Rosie's voice, and she would run into his arms for a cuddle; his eyes shining. Yet Maudie knew he could not see Rosie, and he could not see her when she pinched Sammy and made him cry! But she had to be careful if her father was in the same room for he heard every sound; even if she made no sound he knew somebody was there.

'Who is it? Why don't you speak? It's Maudie, I suppose? Teasing me, again, eh, Maudie?'

Then her stifled giggle would explode and she would run away.

Both girls were small and wiry like their mother, and would have been equally at home in the Old Kent Road. The boys favoured Tom.

'Four kids is enough in this poky little plyce, but I reckon I'll have to manage if I get caught again,' Ruby told Tom. 'There's nothing you and me can do abaht it,' she concluded, with the accustomed resignation of her day and age.

'No, my girl, nothing!' Tom agreed, with manly indulgence!

The card at Christmas was the only indication that Gordon was still living in Paris, but since he had never disclosed his address, Annie could not write to him. This youngest son

85

was so much like his father, in looks and character, it had not surprised Annie that he chose to live in this way. But a mother cannot put a child out of her mind, and she often thought of this wayward son. She wondered whether he had been more successful as an artist in his adopted country. According to Dick, there was an 'Artists' Colony' in Paris, so Gordon would be living in the right environment, and even if he was poor, he would not starve.

This unconventional way of life was alien to her other sons, and Gordon's name was rarely mentioned. Looking back on that early tragedy, and its inevitable consequences, Annie remembered how Gordon had been driven away like his father, *for the same reason*. 'Like father, like son,' they said of Teddy Parsons and young Gordon, but to seduce Stan's wife, Kathie, when he was serving his country in the Great War, was more than enough to cause this lasting rift in the family. Responsibility was a burden. Both her husband and her youngest son chose to run away rather than face it.

Somebody had to behave decently, Annie told herself. Her sturdy independence had kept the wolf from the door when the boys were young, yet her good example had not rubbed off on Teddy and Gordon. It had been brushed aside. They had not listened to her advice, or cared about such fundamental issues as honest work, and honest dealings, for they had no scruples in helping themselves – even to defiling the sanctity of marriage. Such wonderful plans, such a bright future Annie had visualised for her boys, but the War had played havoc with many a mother's hopes. So much heartbreak and separation. They had to build a new world with the remnants of the old.

Now a new generation was growing up. Grandchildren brought joy again, and empty places were filled.

Lucy had soon settled down at the village school, for she

enjoyed learning. At the age of seven she was a bright, intelligent child in the First Standard; her little world secure. The death of Grandfather Pearce during that first year at school had not greatly disturbed this safe little world, for she had not seen him for some time, since he spent the last six months of his life in a nursing home at Tunbridge Wells.

At home and at school Lucy accepted her cherished role as right and proper, because she *was* Lucy Parsons. In her white starched pinafore with the Alice band on her long, straight hair, she still kept that *Alice-in-Wonderland* appeal. On Sundays she wore a bow of ribbon to match her frock. Her shining hair was Annie's pride, and joy.

Dick had been persuaded back into the hop-gardens that year, when Lucy was seven. He hadn't picked hops since he was a boy, and still held the same opinion that it was a hard way to earn a few pounds, but it served a good purpose in keeping him outdoors during the six weeks' vacation from teaching. His health had been permanently impaired by gas poisoning in the trenches of Flanders.

It pleased Annie to have her tall, distinguished son picking hops in the same bine, and it pleased Lucy to have his company. If they sometimes wandered away together and disappeared into the shady woods on a hot September afternoon, Annie would understand they had gone in search of some diversion in the shape of nature study. Perched on the edge of the bin she would carry on picking quietly and methodically. Annie would never be an expert picker, and her daily toll of bushels, even with the help of Dick, was below average compared to the other women in the home-pickers' set who had been picking hops since early childhood. But she enjoyed this seasonal migration of families from the village to the farms. For Annie it was a holiday – the only kind of holiday a working mother could expect – once she had finished child-bearing, with its customary ten-days' confinement to bed.

87

At the adjoining bine she had the lively company of Ruby and her children. She could watch Tom pulling the bines, escorted by young Rosie, happy in his rightful element, proud to be doing a man's work again. And she could watch little Sammy stumbling over the clods with his puny legs in irons. She had known that Christmas, two years ago, that the child was suffering from some obscure disease of which she had no knowledge. No child of three would lie on the sofa on Christmas Day unless he was feeling poorly. Sammy was flushed with fever all that day, and she had nursed him on her lap in the afternoon, while Stan and Dick played Ludo, Snap and Happy Families with the three little girls. Then she had persuaded Tom and Ruby to leave him overnight, and he shared the big marriage bed with Lucy. She had two small grandchildren snuggling into her warm, motherly bosom that night, but Sammy had been hot and restless, and kept her awake.

The following day Stan had turned out the old push-chair with the carpet seat, brushed and oiled it. Sammy's legs were wrapped in a shawl, and she trundled him to the village to see the new young doctor who had a good reputation for diagnosing the ailments of children. It was more than twelve months before Sammy would see his home again. His baby brother would be running about on a pair of sturdy legs, while he stumbled around clumsily in the irons they had put on his legs in hospital. He had infantile paralysis.

Ruby had wept when Stan cycled to the farm to tell them what had happened.

'I should have known it were something more serious than growing pains, when he kept falling abaht,' she sobbed. 'He's not going to die, is he, Stan?'

'No, he won't die, but he will be badly handicapped, for he may have to wear irons on his legs for the rest of his life,' Stan explained kindly. 'Somebody will have to push him to school later, in the push-cart, but it shouldn't be too difficult to find an older girl willing to do this, with so many children passing this way. They will probably be fighting over the job of pushing Sammy to school.'

'Rosie will push him. She's a good girl and fond of her little brothers,' said Tom, decidedly. He was not feeling too happy about the future. How would Ruby cope with two handicapped people in the family? He could foresee the child getting all the attention. For several years he had expected and demanded more than his share of Ruby's attention. He could be jealous of his own children when Ruby's fitful maternity disturbed his self-importance.

Stan was watching his brother's reaction to the news, for that blinded face was more expressive than any sighted face. He was sorry for Ruby, who would be torn apart by the demands of a blind husband and a crippled child. What a hard life she had chosen with Tom, but time enough to worry about Sammy's homecoming, for he was expected to be away for a year, or longer.

The immediate problem was to arrange for Ruby to visit him in hospital, and the farmer's wife agreed to release her one day a week. Ruby would travel in the carter's van to Tunbridge Wells, and Annie would accompany her. They would take Charlie, but there was no extra charge for a child who could be nursed. Once again Annie's little nest egg for a rainy day would be used to pay for the journey, and the gifts they would take. They couldn't go empty-handed to visit a child in hospital.

Stan was glancing round the cluttered room, comparing it to his own home. The baby was crawling on the floor, bare-bottomed, with a dribbling chin. Dead ashes filled the grate from yesterday's fire. Ruby was a poor housewife, but what could you expect with babies coming along so quickly, a blind husband and the obligation of all farm labourer's wives to help with the seasonal work in the hop-gardens and fruit picking.

'Try not to worry,' Stan was saying. 'Sammy is in the right place to get all the professional care he needs. This is not something that can be treated at home by the local doctor. It takes a specialist.'

'But why does it have to happen to our Sammy?' Ruby wailed. 'He's done nothing to deserve it. It's not fair!'

That was a question Stan could not answer. He squeezed her thin shoulders affectionately, and promised to keep in touch.

'I'll make him a toy. Something small he can hold in his hands in bed.'

'And I'll tyke him some sweets and apples, and anythink else I can find. The poor little bugger,' sniffed Ruby. 'It's a shyme for such a little kid to be made to suffer. Don't you think so, Tom?'

'Of course it is, but none of us asks for what we get in the way of suffering. It's not so bad in hospital, I reckon, with all the other children in the ward. They will make a great fuss of him. He won't want to come home, you'll see!'

And Tom was proved right, for the crowded farm cottage could not be compared with the warmth and comfort, the good food, and the loving care he had received in hospital. He missed the young nurses and the doctors whose faces had become so familiar. His father was a stranger, quick-tempered and sullen, and Sammy was afraid of him.

When his sisters were at school and both parents working, he was obliged to play with Charlie in a corner of the big farm kitchen. They were penned in like sheep but Charlie could climb over the barrier. When nobody came to take him to the lavatory, he wet his pants and was scolded. In hospital you never had to wait. Somebody ran quickly to the rescue when you called. They understood. They understood *everything* about a

90

little boy with crippled legs.

Miss Price, Annie's loyal friend of the Merton Hall days, always paid a visit to Annie and her family in the hop-garden one afternoon during the last week of picking. She was not a young woman now, for another generation of children were growing up.

It was Ruby who was dragging the iron-wheeled pram-cart, in which, so long ago, Annie's boys had taken their turn to ride, two by two, the long two miles to the farm. Now it was Sammy and Charlie who rode down the lane from the farm cottage. The pram-cart was loaded with boys, the provisions for the day, and old coats for the children to cover their heads in the rain. Why did children only cover their heads in the rain? Annie wondered. Annie was a little ashamed of her four grandchildren, for the home-pickers' children were expected to set a good example in cleanliness and good behaviour. Ruby's children came to the hop-garden unwashed, eating their breakfast of bread and dripping. Lucy would stare at her cousins with the superior air of a child who knows she is looking her best, and behaving like a little lady. Very reluctantly she had to accept the fact she had to share her Granny with these four young cousins for all the six weeks of hop-picking.

'She's *our* Gran and don't you forget it!' Rosie would remind her, with her mother's sharpness.

But this year was different, for Lucy had her father picking hops in Granny's bin. She would stand beside him and share the bine that was flung across the bin when she felt like helping, but always she wore an old pair of cotton gloves that once had been worn to church on summer Sundays. Annie and Dick would exchange an indulgent smile, but make no comment, for they were familiar with the child's fastidiousness. Rosie and Maudie would tease their cousin, and Ruby laughed the loud, rollicking

91

Cockney laugh she had never lost. Lucy flushed and hung her head until they had finished with her for some other diversion.

It was usually the Cockney families who provided the most hilarious diversions. Ruby would leave the bin, snatch up the baby and run to join the people she still regarded as her own people. All the year she looked forward to this seasonal invasion from Stepney and Lime-house, the Elephant and Castle and the Old Kent Road. For these few short weeks, she enjoyed their lively companionship, and her children played with Cockney children. She bawled all the old music hall songs, while Rosie and Maudie picked up the new songs. If only Ruby had been allowed to pick in one of the sets with the London families, there would have been less embarrassment for Annie, but tradition was strong in the hop-garden, and those who worked for the farmer had perforce to pick in the home-pickers' set.

As for Tom's reactions at this period, he made no secret of the fact that he would be glad when his wife's people went back where they belonged. Every year the same question troubled him – would Ruby be strong enough to resist the urge to climb on the last wagon to the station? His hold on her tightened as the picking season drew to a close. In the marriage bed, the tears he shed at the thought of losing her were genuine enough. Life without this cheerful, indomitable little woman would be intolerable. He could not force her to stay from a sense of duty, for Ruby had no sense of duty. She lived by instinct, and her feelings were not governed by logic. There was a childishness about her still that found its echo in Rosie and Maudie. Ruby was 'our Mum', but she was also someone who could laugh and cry with them, as well as swear and slap. 'Our Mum' was afraid of cows, darkness and spiders, but this they could understand for they felt the same way. She was not afraid of their blind father or his violent temper, for she knew how to manage him!

'Miss Price is coming to see us this afternoon,' Annie told her grandchildren in the dinner hour. One by one she had wiped the four grubby faces and sticky hands with a damp flannel she kept for that purpose, then she tidied hair and changed Charlie's wet pants.

'Who's Miss Price?' Sammy demanded.

Annie explained patiently, for the child had forgotten so much in all the months he had been away.

'What will she have for me, then?' was a natural question after all the spoiling in hospital.

'Sweets and books,' said Lucy promptly, who had seen much more of Miss Price than her cousins.

'Don't want books, want sweets!' Sammy was not an easy child to handle since he had come home. They could not know how sadly he was missing the big, bright hospital ward that had been his home for so long.

'You can have my sweets if you like,' said Rosie, generously.

'All right then,' Sammy agreed, not in the least surprised.

'Like father, like son,' Annie was thinking, for the handicapped child was already demanding his share of attention and the first choice from her own basket in the dinner hour, when the two families sat down together.

Dick was quietly amused by the behaviour of his brother's family, but secretly comparing them with his own small daughter. For her sake he had been persuaded into this marathon task of picking hops for six weeks. Never again, he promised himself. There must be more interesting and better-paid jobs for school teachers in the long summer vacation. Next year he would make enquiries early, study the advertisements in *The Times* and *Tele-*

93

graph. How did other married teachers, with home responsibilities, pass the time fruitfully? He was wondering, as he drained the last dregs of tea from his mother's flask, yawned and stretched on the old coat spread over the heap of stripped bines. Lucy was tucked in the crook of his arm, sucking a peppermint, and he smiled down at her, his thoughts still persisting with an alternative plan for next summer. There was hotel work, of course, in the holiday season. They both would benefit from the sea air, and Lucy would love the beach. He would have to find a sensible young girl to look after her while he was working. They would stay in lodgings, with a landlady to cook for them. Now the idea was taking shape in his mind. He would talk about it later, when they were alone together. She would be delighted at the prospect of getting away from the hop-garden next year, for they both had found the six weeks interminable.

'Daddy,' she whispered.

'Yes, pet?'

'How many more days?'

'Three.'

'Counting today?'

'No, after today.'

She sighed, and he bent to kiss the tip of her nose.

'Think of something nice, then the time will pass quickly.'

'What shall I think about?'

'There's the Tunbridge Wells treat, before we go back to school.'

She sat up with eagerness. 'I'd forgotten.' She counted on her fingers. 'Two shillings pocket money to spend – Woolworths – dinner at Weeks' Restaurant – tea in the Pantiles – and –'

'There and back by train,' he prompted.

'There and back by train,' she echoed, wriggling with excitement. 'Oh, Daddy! I wish it was today.'

'It would be over too soon.'

'Yes,' she agreed, doubtfully.

'Me and Maudie is going to Tunbridge Wells after the 'opping. Our Mum's going to take us,' Rosie interrupted.

Ruby looked surprised. It was the first she had heard of it. They couldn't afford treats. The hop-picking money would pay the bills that were owing in the village. She just couldn't make ends meet.

Rosie was perched on the edge of the bin, her arm round Charlie. Her eyes were pleading. She was a good girl.

'I'll take yer,' Ruby said – and added, as a sharp reminder 'by carrier, mind. Train fares is too much, an' it's three miles to the station.'

Rosie nodded and kicked her heels, nearly tipping Charlie into the bin, half filled with hops and a good sprinkling of leaves where Tom had added his small contribution. Maudie would scramble about in the bin later and pick them out. It was easier than upsetting Tom by telling him he was a dirty picker. There were some jobs a blind man should never attempt, and picking hops was one. Ruby wished he would be satisfied with pulling the bines and holding up the sack for the farmer when he measured out the hops, but Tom was never satisfied with his achievements. He had to keep on attempting the impossible. Everyone said he was marvellous, but they didn't have to live with Tom.

Charlie was wriggling again and Ruby lifted him down. 'If you pee in them clean pants, I'll smack yer bum!' she threatened – and dragged him a few yards down the aisle.

'Oh dear, she's right back to her Cockney talk,' Annie was thinking, as she tidied up the remnants of the meal. Only three more days, thank goodness. It happened every year when Ruby was surrounded by her own people for six long weeks.

95

Dick was watching his mother covertly. How had she managed to keep that serene look through all the troubled years? Such a hard life, bringing up four boys almost single-handed, but she was not one to complain. He remembered the lines of washing in the scullery, the smell of yellow soap and the boiling copper. A small corner of the table in the living-room had been cleared for his school books, but every evening, six days a week, the hot smell of ironing irritated his asthma and made him cough. Now he was struck afresh by her serenity and patience in dealing with Tom's family. Then, they had seldom seen her eyes darkened in anger in their own childhood. It was disconcerting when it happened, whether you were guilty or not. Their boyhood escapades had not angered her, disobedience went unpunished, but lies she could not tolerate. Gordon's petty pilfering had been one of the biggest problems. Tom's blindness had left its mark on her greying head.

When Stan lost his young wife, Kathie, and Gordon disappeared, it had broken her heart, but not her spirit. His own unhappy marriage, the separation and divorce was something beyond her understanding, yet she had welcomed him back with his child. They were not demonstrative, he and Stan. They didn't need to tell her she was still the central figure in their little world. She knew.

So when he spoke to her now, his quiet voice conveyed his thoughts and she turned her head to smile at him.

'We are just going for our usual little walk. We shan't be long,' he said, glancing at his watch. 'Twenty minutes and then back to work!'

He pulled Lucy to her feet and they slipped away together. Rosie looked after them, wistfully, for a moment, then ran to join Tom and the dog, just disappearing into the green tunnel.

'Wait for me, Dad!' she yelled. And Tom spun round,

grinning, and waited.

'Got something for you. Bet you can't guess what it is.'

'Bet you ha'penny I can!'

'Go on then!'

It was a game they often played, and she always won the halfpenny. When she took his hand and closed his palm over a soft, fat 'hop-dog', she shrieked with glee at the face he pulled.

'Caught me again,' he said, and gave her the halfpenny.

'I'll carry it for you, Dad. It's sort of pretty,' she told him.

'Yes, I know.'

It was difficult for a child to understand there had once been a time when he could see.

They walked on together, hand-in-hand, the dog trotting ahead. They were very close. 'He's my dad. He's the best dad in the world,' she thought – and forgot that moment of doubt, watching Uncle Dick with Lucy.

When Dick climbed back over the gate and lifted Lucy down, the scene before him was vividly sketched in the glare of the midday sun. The hop-garden was stripped, but for a couple of acres or so at the bottom left-hand corner. The bins were crowded together now. Gypsies, Cockneys and home-pickers were moving gradually towards the tall hedge that bordered the lane. There was no beauty left in the stripped garden, only the desolation in the heaps of dead bines, and the sun-baked clods.

'All to work!'

That resounding voice had echoed through the wood, and Dick hurried to obey the summons. Children swarmed in the trees and bushes, shouting defiance to that echoing voice. Lucy was also reluctant to leave the shady wood for the sun scorched hop-garden, and another long afternoon. Her mouth was pouting as Dick lifted her over the gate.

97

'We mustn't let the side down, pet. Granny will be expecting us,' he coaxed.

On the far side of the clearing they could see Tom and the dog, waiting for Rosie who was gathering the last of the hazel nuts from the bushes. Sammy was teasing the dog as usual, and the dog was barking. Groups of women were drifting back to the bins. Babies were dropped into pram-carts. Cockney mothers were yelling – 'Bertie!' – 'Katie!' – 'Johnny!' – 'Maree!'. Now the wood was silent.

'*We* know where they are, don't we, Daddy?' Lucy whispered.

Dick nodded, and pointed to the wide open gate. 'Look! Here comes Miss Price. She wasn't expected so early.'

The frisky young pony was tossing its head nervously. Miss Price stood up in the trap and tightened her hold on the reins. The mare that had pulled the trap since the days of the nursery governess had died of old age, and the pony was difficult to handle. They both were nervous, and the woman's nervousness was transmitted to the animal.

Annie had heard the clatter of wheels at the gate, and hurried across the garden, holding Maudie by the hand. Ruby snatched up Charlie. Any diversion was welcome in this last week of picking. Rosie had disappeared in her search for nuts. Sammy was still teasing the dog, and its sharp yapping startled the pony. Only Ruby saw Tom push the child roughly away. Only Ruby and Dick saw him stumbling over the clods in the path of the frisky pony.

Ruby screamed and ran. Sammy stood transfixed for a few seconds. Then he started to shout and wave his arms. He expected the pony to stop, like a cow, when he waved his arms and shouted. But the pony didn't stop.

'Stand still, sweetheart,' said Dick, quietly, as he dropped Lucy's hand and ran. His long, loping strides soon out-distanced Ruby, with her heavy burden. As Sammy fell sprawling, Dick was there to fling himself on the child, under the prancing hooves.

Miss Price was pulling on the reins with all her puny strength, the pony rearing and snorting with fright. Now the clearing was suddenly swarming with screaming women and children were scrambling eagerly back through all the gaps in the hedges. Ruby dropped Charlie in the dust, ignored his yells of protest, and ran, sobbing hysterically.

'Sammy! Sammy!'

When the child wriggled out, screaming with fright, but unhurt, she snatched him up with a passionate hug, and had no thought for the man who had saved him.

Annie was the first to reach that still figure. She fell on her knees, calling his name, but he made no answer. Her hop-stained hand trembled over the swelling bruise on his temple. She knew he was dead, even before the Red Cross nurse confirmed it.

'Dick,' she moaned. 'Dick!', stroking his face.

The pandemonium all about her hardly reached her shocked senses. She was aware only of Dick, and the swelling bruise.

Now the farmer had quieted the pony, and his wife was trying to revive poor Miss Price with sips of brandy from a small flask.

Tom stood like a statue, with the dog, his lifted, listening face tortured by fear. What had happened? Why didn't Rosie come back?

On the other side of the clearing, a little girl in a white, starched pinafore and a straw hat, stood waiting. 'Stand still, sweetheart.' That's what he said. Lucy had always been an obedient child. She was standing still.

Only when Dick's slight body had been borne away on a trestle by two farm-hands, was Annie mindful of the child. She stood up, swaying, and looked about her with anguished eyes.

'Lucy? – Where's Lucy?' she asked.

Some two hundred yards away, a tiny, solitary figure stood framed against the tall hedges. And Annie ran, gasping and sobbing.

'Lucy! Lucy! Come to Granny!'

The child stood motionless, and when Annie's arms enfolded her, there was no response – no sound, no word, no warmth in the stiff little body, Annie was hugging to her breast. They stood there locked together, only a few yards from the gate Dick had climbed so easily to lift Lucy down. Annie was choked with tears, the child's eyes were dry in her chalk-white face. 'I must get her home, she's terribly shocked, poor mite,' Annie was thinking. With an arm about her shoulders, she led the way across the wide expanse of desolation exposed to the blank stares of the curious children and the silent groups of women. Some were hugging the children they had threatened to murder only a short time ago. They followed the sad little procession through the gate, down the lane to the farmhouse. The farmer was leading the pony now. His wife sat in the trap, supporting Miss Price, still faint with shock.

Behind Annie and Lucy, a group of children followed silently, awed by the solemn pace of the little procession. Maudie was clutching Rosie's hand.

'Is Uncle Dick deaded?' she asked.

Rosie nodded.

'How does he get deaded?' she persisted.

'Mum says the pony kicked him. I never saw nothing. I was over the hedge, looking for nuts.'

'Won't Lucy have a Dad no more?'

'No – Dad?' Rosie gasped. 'I got to go back. I left our Dad in the field!' She dropped her sister's hand and flew back down the lane. Across the clearing she raced, calling as she ran.

100

'Dad! Dad! I'm coming, Dad!'

Tom had not moved. His face was distorted with anger and fear.

'Where have you been? What happened? Why doesn't somebody tell me what's happened?' he demanded savagely.

Rosie flung herself on the solid, sturdy figure and hugged him round the waist. Only an hour ago she had envied Lucy; now her father was dead.

'Oh, Dad! Our Dad! I do love you, honest I do!' she sobbed.

'*What happened?*' Tom shouted, gripping her shoulders.

'It's Uncle Dick – he's dead,' she gulped.

'Dead?' echoed Tom in a horrified whisper. 'How – how did it happen?'

'Mum says he was kicked by the pony. Our Sammy wasn't hurt. Sammy's all right. They've took Uncle Dick to the farm. Gran and Lucy was there. I come back to fetch you, Dad.'

'Where's your mother?'

'I don't know. I think she went back to the bin.'

'Take me home, Rosie.'

'Yes, Dad.'

The sad little procession had disappeared. They walked down the lane in silence, hand-in-hand. The sadness was all about them, and it followed them to the empty cottage.

'Nobody here, so they must be still down in the garden,' said Tom.

'Yes, Dad,' Rosie agreed. 'Shall I make a cup of tea?'

'Yes.'

He followed her to the kitchen, filled a small tin bowl with water and gave the dog a drink. Then he stood in the open doorway, his face lifted, listening, but nobody came near them. As they skirted the farmhouse, Rosie had seen

Maudie with the group of children in the yard. The doors were closed. There was nothing to be seen. She would come home soon.

Rosie filled the special mug that was Dad's mug with hot, strong tea, stirred in two spoonsful of sugar. Then she put the mug in his hand. He stood there, sipping the tea, his eyelids wet with tears, and she started to cry again in sympathy, but did not know what to say to comfort him.

'Why doesn't she come? She must know I would be upset,' he mumbled.

'Everybody's upset, Dad,' she reminded him. 'People was crying all over the place when I come out from the hedge. Did you hear our Mum screaming?'

'I heard.'

'Reckon she thought our Sammy was dead. But it wasn't Sammy. It were Uncle Dick.'

'Tell me again what happened. I can't seem to take it in.'

Perched on the kitchen table, Rosie retold the story, and added, as an afterthought, 'Wonder who'll be taking Standard Six now Uncle Dick's dead?'

Tom made no answer. His sun-tanned face looked greyish in the harsh light of the sun. He loved the sun and always moved towards it. Rosie knew every expression on that dear, familiar face, its light and shade. But now, for the first time, she saw his face stricken and tortured with shock, the furrows deep on his forehead, the eyes dulled. This man was a stranger, and he did not want her. He wanted their Mum.

When she slid off the table and went past him, he seemed not to notice she had gone. The dog lay stretched at his feet, gazing upon him with pleading, limpid eyes. Rosie walked slowly back down the lane and leaned on the gate, staring at the spot where the pony had kicked Uncle Dick. Nothing had changed. The heaps of dead bines were still undisturbed, the sun-baked clods were still there. And away in the

102

distance, little groups of women were picking hops in the bins as though nothing had happened. Perhaps it was just a bad dream?

She shivered in the hot sun, and went in search of her mother. Then she saw her coming away from the rest of the pickers, dragging the pram-cart with the two heavy children, and ran to meet her.

'Dad wants you, Mum!' she gasped.

'Let 'im wait!' Ruby snapped impatiently.

Rosie stared. Dad was never kept waiting. Dad came first, always. They all knew he had to be first, even little Charlie.

'Dad's crying,' she said.

'Then 'e's not the only one!' Ruby retorted. ''ere, give us an 'and with this 'ere cart. I've just abaht 'ad as much as I can stand for one dye!'

'Yes, Mum,' said Rosie, obediently, and pushed from the back with all her strength.

There was going to be a row – a wopping big row. She could feel it inside. Mum was mad at Dad, but why? It wasn't his fault Uncle Dick was dead.

'I never got no sweets. Miss Price never gave me no sweets!' Sammy was grumbling.

'Serves you right!' Rosie told him, spitefully, and went on pushing.

When they passed the farmyard, Maudie left the other children and ran to join them. One glance at her mother's glowering face was enough to warn her that trouble was brewing. She slipped to the back of the pram-cart and whispered, 'What's up with our Mum?' but got no answer from Rosie. So she ran on ahead, looking for a new diversion in a day that had brought such a sudden end to picking hops.

She was too small to stand at the bin, so she filled Gran's big black umbrella, once in the morning and again in the afternoon. Today she hadn't even started on the afternoon umbrella, and nobody had bothered to remind her, with all the commotion over Sammy and Uncle Dick. Maudie was always looking for a chance to escape the clutching hold of her family, and she could disappear as suddenly and completely as a rabbit in a burrow. Maudie felt no obligation to a blind father or a little crippled brother, and had none of her sister's sensitiveness to their suffering. Hard slaps from their Mum served only to induce rebellion. When she was expected to cry, she laughed. When she was told to amuse her little brothers, she teased them, and ran away. Her cheeky defiance of both parents in the past few months seemed to alienate her from the rest of the family. Uncle Dick was deaded, but she hadn't known him properly, not like Uncle Stan. Now she crept up silently to the back of the cottage and hid in the privy.

Standing on the seat, she could see our Dad in the doorway, and she didn't like the look of him one little bit. She would keep out of his way.

The pram-cart rattled up the lane and stopped at the gate. Through the air-vent at the top of the privy door, she could hear every word that passed between her parents, and she could see her two little brothers toddling past to play in the back garden.

Rosie was crying again, and Maudie hissed to attract her attention. Then she slid into the privy and joined her sister on the seat. What was there to cry about, Maudie wondered. Rows were commonplace, and she quite enjoyed them now she was big enough not to mind all the shouting and swearing. Our Mum always had the last word anyway!

'Is that you, Rube?' Tom called out anxiously.

'It's me all right!' Ruby snapped, as she walked towards him, burdened with old coats, bags and baskets.

'Where have you been?' he demanded, truculently.

'Where jew think I've been? – pickin' the 'ops! Some-

104

body's got ter pick 'em if we're goin' ter get finished by Sat'dye.'

'But I wanted you, Rube. You just left me standing there, not knowing what was happening. It was a mean thing to do.'

'Mean?' she shouted. 'You was the mean one, Tom Parsons! I see'd it all, an' yer can't fool me with yer soft talk! Blimey! It's a bloody miracle they wasn't both killed! – *an' all your fault!* You shoved 'im away, the poor little bugger, an' you've been shovin' 'im away ever since 'e come 'ome from the 'orspital. One of these dyes there's goin' ter be a nasty accident, I told meself, many a time. Well, I were right, weren't I?' She was all Cockney now – the same vulgar little spitfire he first met in the hop-garden that September before the war.

Tom flinched at the unexpected attack when he had expected sympathy and understanding. He could find no words to answer her. His fault? Is that what they were saying? Oh, my God! It was true he felt no love for Sammy, only resentment because the child demanded his share of attention, and Ruby made such a fuss of him.

'Well, I ain't puttin' up with it no more. I'm fed ter the teeth! I'm clearin' aht, Satdye!' she hurled the threat like an arrow, and he staggered, as though the missile had struck him, reaching out to her imploringly.

'No, Rube, you can't mean it?'

'I mean it, Tom. I been wantin' ter go back 'ome wiv me own people every year when the 'oppin' is finished, and yer know I 'ave. This tyme I'm goin' and I'm tyking Sammy and Charlie. The girls will look after yer. Rosie's a good girl, an' Maudie's not ser bad if you let 'er alone. You'll just 'ave ter manage.'

The two girls were clutching each other in the privy. Rosie was crying miserably.

'She don't mean it, Rose. She's just mad at our Dad,' her

105

sister reminded her.

'She *do* mean it, Maud,' sniffed Rosie. 'But how can she blame our Dad when he can't *see*? It's not fair.'

'Our Dad don't have to see to give our Sammy a clout,' said Maudie, sensibly. She often seemed to be the elder sister now. She saw things differently, and was not so inclined to make allowances for blindness. All her short life had been lived in the orbit of this stormy relationship between her parents. Tempers were frayed and nerves near to breaking point. Neither had really adjusted to an alien world in the several years they had lived together as man and wife. But they were her parents, and Maudie accepted them.

'If our Mum goes to London, I'm not staying here with our Dad,' she declared, defiantly. 'You can look after our Dad. He likes you best, don't he?'

Rose nodded. 'But I loves our Mum. I want we should all be together,' she whimpered.

The gypsies left early that Saturday morning, and went away quietly. The smell of fried onions and fat pork still lingered, and their fires were still smouldering as they left the field. By mid-morning the last of the wagons trundled down the lane, piled high with Cockney families, their dogs, cats and canaries, bundles of bedding, pots and pans. They were shouting the music hall songs they had been shouting for six weeks, and calling out in shrill excitement to the farmer and his wife.

'Ta-Ta, luv! See yer next 'oppin'. Look after yerselves!'

All the local children trailed behind. They would ride back on the empty wagon. Rosie and Maudie were there with the rest, but Mum was not on the wagon, and Dad had not been seen since breakfast. The boys had been left with a neighbour while Ruby said her goodbyes. They were perched on the wall, waiting to wave as the wagons pulled out of the yard.

Rosie had been doubtful about joining the other farm children on this annual trek to the station, for nothing had been settled and she was worried. But it was fun, and she couldn't bear to miss it. So she went along with the rest. It was a little over three miles to the station, but all the children were accustomed to walking long distances.

A mile from the farm, in the opposite direction, Tom was trudging along with the dog, a knapsack on his back. For three days he had pleaded with Ruby, wept and cursed, but her mind was made up. He had slipped away quietly, followed the path across the field, and climbed over the stile. He had no plans, but he had to get away. Ruby would take all the children to London when she discovered he was missing.

He had been walking now for an hour or more, and every step was taking him farther away from the place he loved beyond all else – the farm that had been his home since he was a lad of fourteen, but for that period in the Army, and the shattering experience of his blindness.

Choked with tears, his keen ear detected the sound of running footsteps even before they reached the bend in the lane. They came nearer, then a voice, sharp with anger and anxiety, called after him, 'Tom! Tom! Wait for me, can't yer!'

He stopped and turned to face her.

'Where jew think you're goin', Tom Parsons?' she demanded.

'Away,' he said. 'I'm no good to anyone around here, so I'm clearing out.'

She flung her arms about his neck and burst into tears.

'You come on back, you silly old bugger! Jew 'ear me?'

Tom grinned as his arms closed round her thin shoulders.

'You're the boss, my love,' he said.

107

Chapter Five

All through the month of October the child seemed to exist in a state of shocked suspension, walking, talking, eating, sleeping, with the automatic movements of a puppet. Neither Annie's gentleness, nor Stan's devoted patience could reach beyond the emptiness of those dark eyes.

The young doctor advised Annie to keep the child at home for time could heal a mental as well as a physical illness.

'Let her do as she likes. It's not medicine she needs, Mrs Parsons. All she needs is a good cry.'

But Lucy had not cried. Dry-eyed she had followed that still form on the hurdle down the lane to the farm, clutching Annie's hand. Dry-eyed she had been driven home in the trap by Miss Price, some time later, after drinking a cup of tea. Uncle Stan had nursed her all evening like a baby on the sagging old sofa, till it was time for bed, then carried her upstairs. For the first time since her own children were small, Annie's warm, comforting bosom found no response, and it saddened her. No two people could have been more loving than Dick's mother and brother. They missed his quiet, gentle presence about the house, for Dick had seldom asserted himself, even as a boy.

'My clever son,' Annie had called her second boy. She had been so proud when he passed the scholarship to Grammar School. All the books in the house belonged to Dick, and Lucy, for he encouraged her to read. He was happy and content with his teaching post at the village school, though he could have earned a higher salary else-where. It suited him to be living under his mother's peace-ful roof again, after the few disturbing years of a troubled marriage. Their little world had seemed complete, lacking nothing in affection and companionship.

Now it was shattered. It was impossible to believe that Dick would never again stand blinking in the bright sun-light, polishing his glasses; never again wind the hand-knitted muffler about his neck to keep the cold from his weak chest; never again read Lucy's bedtime story; never again advise his mother on the best way to invest her small savings, or balance her accounts. A dozen times a day they expected to see him, to hear his quiet voice. But he did not come, and nobody could ever fill the gap he had left in that small family circle.

Stan was doing his best to play the role of a second father to Lucy, sparing neither time nor money to induce the child to take an interest in her surroundings again, but he had not succeeded. Even the new bicycle he could ill afford now that Dick's salary had been curtailed, brought no response, other than a polite 'Thank you, Uncle Stan'. The piquant little face that once had been lively with pleasure at every small gift had lost its radiance. Stan had taught her to ride, but she accomplished it with the stilted formality of a doll set in motion to perform certain tricks.

The music teacher who was teaching Lucy to play the piano did not complain that her pupil was careless or lazy, only that she lacked interest.

'Poor child. We must be patient. It's been a terrible shock,' she told Annie.

But the days and the weeks went by with no sign of im-provement. They could not leave Lucy, even for an hour, and she spent her days following Annie around the house, or watching Stan in the workshop. Love and compassion flooded his being when his eyes met the eyes of the child across the work bench. If only he could see a tiny spark of the old eagerness to lend a hand! If only he could be the one to ignite that spark!

'What more can we do, Mum?' he asked. 'There must be something more she needs that you and I have not been able to give her. I wish I knew.'

It had been a sad disappointment that she accepted the new bicycle as though it had cost only a few shillings.

When school was mentioned, Lucy shook her head, but the School Attendance Officer calling for the second time, insisted that Annie must be firm with the child. She must return to school after Christmas.

'The longer she stays away, the harder it will be. You are making a rod for your own back, Mrs Parsons,' he pointed out with some severity.

'It's because my son was a teacher and they went to school together,' Annie reminded him, quietly.

'That has already been taken into consideration. We cannot allow any further indulgence. Good-day to you,' was his last word on the matter.

Annie watched him go with a sinking heart. She and Stan had been defeated in their joint efforts to restore the child's unbalanced mind. Tears, the natural outlet for an unhappy child, would cleanse and heal this sickness, but Lucy did not cry. Where have we failed? Annie asked herself, for it was not the first time she and Stan had been defeated by some force beyond their understanding. They had failed with Tom when he came home blinded, after his year of readjustment in hospital and hostel. Tom had resented all their careful arrangements for his comfort and safety. He did not want security. He only wanted to go his own way, regardless of risk. His restlessness and his disagreeable temper had wrecked their peaceful home life. But Ruby had known how to cope with Tom – could still cope, in her own rough fashion.

110

'Time would heal,' the young doctor had assured her, but that was three months ago.

Stan had fixed a saddle on the bar of his bicycle. He would take Lucy to school and collect her at four o'clock. Annie would have liked the child to come home to dinner, but it was not fair to Stan to expect him to leave his work again at midday. Besides, as he pointed out with kind insistence, Lucy could refuse to go back to school in the afternoon and there would be more trouble with the Attendance Officer and a fine to pay.

'If we had our way, Mum, we should let her stay at home, but that wouldn't be right, to deprive her of schooling, for Dick was keen on her education. We're a couple of softies, you and me, and we've always spoiled her. We shall go on spoiling her, but now we have to abide by the rules, or break the law.'

Stan was right, of course, and Annie could see the sense of it. Once a day was distressing enough, and Lucy's pathetic little face brought a lump to the throat, and tears to her eyes. She felt the child's resentment in the stiff little body, as she buttoned up her coat and arranged the new tammy on her plaited hair. It was scarlet, and it had a tassel, with a matching scarf and mittens. Rosie and Maudie had been given similar sets of hand-knitted woollies for Christmas, for Annie was careful not to discriminate between her grandchildren when they all were together on Christmas Day. Children were quick to notice any favouritism, though Tom's girls had been reminded that Lucy had a right to expect something special in the way of presents this year on account of losing her father. They had saved up their halfpennies and bought their cousin a box of plasticine from the bazaar, but Lucy did not care for it – too messy and smelly for her fastidious taste. But it was useful to amuse Charlie while the other children were playing

'Ludo', 'Snakes and Ladders' and 'Snap'.

Annie's thoughts followed Stan and Lucy to school that first day. She wondered if this drastic step towards a normal life would have an even more serious effect on the child. Surely nothing could be worse for a little girl of seven, than this state of being only half alive?

In all her years of being associated with children, Annie had never known a similar case. She wondered how the Superintendent of the Girls' Home would have dealt with such a child – sternly, no doubt. She sighed and wished she knew more about the mind of a child and its complexities. Nobody could accuse her of neglecting the child's body. Even when times were hard, she had fed her boys with good, nourishing food, and thanks to Miss Price, they had always been well clothed. Early to bed in a well ventilated room, and plenty of sleep. Sound principles for healthy young bodies. She had not punished her children, for her memories of her own harsh childhood were still vivid, and she had not enforced obedience. Honesty she had expected, and only Gordon had let her down. Yet, looking back, she knew her concern for their bodies had left no time to cultivate an understanding of all the interesting developments in four healthy young minds.

Even Stan, her first-born, so like her in character and temperament, had not turned to her for advice in that terrible moment of discovering the truth about Gordon and Kathie. He had found his own salvation, eventually, in the organisation and management of a Boy Scout troop in the village. But it was many a long day before their close relationship had been restored.

Dick had always been too clever for her, and she was a little shy of him.

Tom, the sturdiest of her four boys, had given her some anxious moments, but this was only to be expected in a normal healthy boy. She had coped with all his escapades and accidents, but she had not been wise enough to cope with his blindness. It still rankled that she had failed to make contact with her handicapped son in his hour of greatest need.

As for Gordon, her youngest, the only time she had really enjoyed him was that all too short period before he started school. Such deceptive innocence in those blue eyes, had brought nothing but heartache. He was Teddy's son. 'You don't understand,' he had accused her, and it was true. How could she recognise creative talent in all his quaint little pictures?

Now she was saddened by her failure with Lucy, and blamed herself afresh for her lack of understanding.

Lucy's little dinner box hung on the handlebars in a string bag. She would pick at the dainty sandwiches Annie had provided, and Maudie would finish them with relish after the thick slices of bread and jam that Ruby had provided. One of the senior girls would make hot cocoa, and the little girls would fight for a place near the big coke stove.

Frozen snow was banked on either side of the road, for the horse-drawn plough had been out early to clear a path down the High Street.

Lucy shivered as Stan settled her on the saddle, and Annie kissed her tenderly, then stood at the gate to wave. For the past two years she had stood there, watching her clever son on his way to teach the Sixth Standard, and the child walking proudly beside her father, holding his hand, turning back to wave happily till they turned the corner. Today she did not turn her head, and Stan was too preoccupied steering the bike on the icy road.

Annie went slowly back down the path Stan had cleared of snow, forlorn and saddened by the child's misery. A bright fire lit the low-ceilinged room, and flames danced on the dark oak beams. The stove shone black as the coal in the scuttle, and the firelight was reflected in the polished steel fender. It was a homely room and somewhat shabby now.

Haunted by the recent memory of a pathetic little face, suddenly plain with the severity of the compulsory plaits, Annie had no heart to clear the table and wash the dishes. She sank wearily on the sofa and stared into the fire, waiting for Stan to come back. Soon she heard the scrape of his boots at the back door, and he came in, looking pinched with the cold, blowing on his hands, for he would not wear gloves.

Squatting beside her he held his hands to the blazing fire, and she asked quietly, 'What happened?'

'Tom's girls were waiting at the school gate, and when I lifted Lucy down, they each took a hand and led her away across the playground. I was going to take her into the classroom the first day, but they really took over and as she made no fuss and didn't look back to see if I was following, I let her go.'

'Rosie and Maudie will look after her. They are good girls. And Ruby will have told them to look after her. Remember how good they were at Christmas, waiting on her hand and foot, and giving her all the precious little bits and pieces from the crackers they usually kept for themselves.'

Stan nodded, but when he turned his face to look at her, Annie could see he was still worried about the child.

'I also remember that she couldn't bear to have Sammy near her, so she does connect him in some way with Dick's death. She saw it happen, as we know, from where she was standing, but who knows what really goes on in her funny little mind?'

'I was thinking about it, Stan, as I sat here waiting for you to come back – the mind of a child, I mean. I'm not very clever at understanding that sort of thing. Shouldn't a mother know by instinct what a child is thinking?'

114

Stan smiled wryly. 'Perhaps it's just as well you don't, for you might get a bit of a shock.'

'But it's not enough to love a child. There must be understanding. That's where I've failed,' she sighed.

Stan's arm gripped her shoulders and he gave her a little shake. 'Don't talk such rubbish! You're the best Mum in the world, and you know it.'

She blinked the tears from her wet eyes and returned the smile. 'Thank you, Stan,' was all she said, but they had never been demonstrative, and to say more would embarrass them both.

Only once before could Annie remember Stan so eloquent in his praise, and she knew what it cost him.

'You'll be glad of another cup of tea before you start work.' She pushed the kettle over the fire, and warmed the old brown teapot that always stood on the hob.

'Nothing like a cup of tea to warm you up. It's perishing cold outside.'

'I've put on the oil stove in the workshop, so it should be warming up out there.'

'Thanks, Mum. It's going to feel strange without Lucy today.'

'Yes, we shall miss her.'

They drank their tea in silence, then Annie cleared the table and carried the dishes to the scullery. Icicles hung from the outside eaves over the frosted window. The water-butt was frozen solid, and she had to smash the ice on the hens' water bowl when she went to the run to feed them. The last of the brussels sprouts had turned black with the frost, and the bushes were draped in a white mantle of snow. The air was keen and stung the face, but Annie was hardened to these bleak winters in her native Kent. She always felt better in the winter months, but drooped in the heat of mid-summer.

'I'll give the boys' room a good turn out. It hasn't been

115

done thoroughly since – since Dick died,' she thought.

Christmas was over, and Lucy back to school, so there was no further excuse to postpone a job she had been secretly dreading since October. 'Besides, it will keep my mind off Lucy,' she told herself, not very convincingly, for she knew the child would be there all day in the back of her mind, and no amount of polishing and scrubbing would dispel the recent memory of that pathetic little face, gazing up at her from under the scarlet tammy.

This child of Dick's – her first grandchild – had taken up so much of her time in the past three months, and now she would have to fill her days with domestic chores, for the garden was frozen as solid as a rock. She could hear Stan busy in his workshop, and that was company. Before she started on the cleaning, she would make a meat pudding and put it on to boil; it would provide a good, nourishing meal for such a cold day, with potatoes baked in their jackets and a few winter greens she had gathered earlier in the week. It was the kind of meal they both enjoyed, but it wouldn't do for Lucy, with her finicky appetite. She would wait and see what the child fancied for her tea when she came home from school – a poached egg on toast, perhaps, or a savoury pancake. Dick's appetite had always required tempting, but he had suffered from asthma. There was really no reason why Lucy should be so finicky, but they had spoiled her from the start in asking her what she would like to eat.

She dusted Dick's books with loving care and tidied his drawer, where he had kept a collection of albums containing stamps, cigarette cards and pressed flowers. His hobbies had been mostly of a sedentary type, because of his studious nature, and she turned over the pages, admiring afresh the neatness of his work and his writing. Now she was choked with tears again, coming upon an unfinished page that would never be completed.

116

In the bottom left hand corner of the drawer she was surprised to find a small bundle of letters fastened with an elastic band, but when she glanced at the signature of the top letter in the bundle, she put the letters hurriedly back, and felt guilty of prying into Dick's privacy. This was the girl her son should have married – his first love – but for the timely and shattering disclosure that she was his half-sister. What nemesis, but Dick had suffered, not Teddy, whose daughter she was.

Teddy had a lot to answer for, one way and another, Annie was thinking, as she closed the drawer.

The little girl in the scarlet tammy ran out of the school gate and darted across the road, missing the big car by a small margin. She stopped dead, stared, wide-eyed with fright, and dodged back towards the safety of the gate.

'STAND STILL! – YOU LITTLE FOOL! – STAND STILL,' a man's voice yelled testily.

The child stopped, as though compelled by something beyond the irritation, then she turned and ran down the road ahead of the car, screaming hysterically, 'Daddy! Daddy! Daddy!'

'Blast!' muttered the man as he pulled into the kerb and scrambled out. Dressed in a long fur coat, fur cap and gauntlets, he was obviously of the upper class and the car was a new model, adding further proof of his wealth. Scooping up the child in his arms, he carried her back to the car and sat down in the passenger seat, trying to calm her. A little group of women had gathered outside the Bazaar – still flaunting the remnants of the Christmas decorations – and they were staring at the man accusingly. A gang of boys had followed the girl from the school gate and were standing about the car in gaping admiration, completely ignoring the girl's crying. With so many sisters, it was no novelty to see a girl in tears, but the car was something big and important to swank about to those who had missed it.

The man soon gave up the attempt to pacify the child, for she was so frightened he could not get through to her. She had buried her face in the soft fur and was clutching him in a frenzy of passionate weeping.

'Good Lord, the kid's a nervous wreck,' he thought, dispassionately. 'Wonder where she belongs – a village child if she attended the village school? Yet she had a certain refinement about her small person, and she was well dressed.

The street was milling with children now, the boys attracted to the car, the girls to the man who owned the car.

'He looks like a Russian count,' one imaginative child whispered.

'So he do,' her friend agreed – sniffing in the keen, wintry blast that struck so chill after the stuffiness of the classroom.

Then a man on a bicycle pulled up at the kerb, propped the bike against the wall and pushed the gaping children aside.

'*Dad!*' he gasped. 'What on earth?' . . .

Teddy smiled disarmingly at his eldest son and privately thought him a poor looking fellow in his cheap overcoat and cloth cap.

'What happened? Is she hurt?' Stan demanded anxiously.

'No, only scared. Who is she?'

'Lucy – Dick's child – your grandchild.' Stan's voice was cold with dislike of this man they all believed dead. Why couldn't he stay decently dead and buried? He reached for the child protectively, but she clung to the comforting warmth of the fur.

Teddy shrugged. 'I seem to be stuck with her, don't I?'

Stan's pinched face flushed angrily. 'You must have scared her pretty badly to upset her like that.'

'I tell you I didn't. Anyway, it wasn't my fault. She ran

118

straight out of the gate and across the road. Fortunately, I was coming up the hill at a steady pace, so I could brake easily. She's such a nervous little thing. I yelled at her to stand still and I believe I called her a little fool, but good heavens man, she wasn't *hurt*.'

'It's my fault. I should have been here to collect her at four o'clock, but I was kept at the last moment by a fussy customer.'

'Customer?' Teddy raised his eyebrows enquiringly.

'Bicycle repairs. Got a workshop in the garden,' said Stan briefly.

So that explained the grimy hands and the cheap clothes. It would be a poor sort of livelihood.

Stan was even more inarticulate than usual, confronted by this extraordinary character who answered to the name of Dad. But he was too concerned for Lucy to bother too much with a father who played such eerie tricks on his family. This man, who had claimed the right of a parent, had never been anything more than a rather disturbing stranger who had left their mother to fend for herself and her four boys for long periods, then suddenly arrived home unannounced, expecting to be welcomed like the Biblical prodigal son.

Stan remembered a time when he was only a little fellow, not understanding what all the fuss was about. 'Teddy Parsons had got a girl of fifteen in the family way, and she had died in childbirth,' – so they said in the village. After that he had gone away again, but it was not the last they saw of him. They looked at each other now, father and son, with hostile eyes, then Teddy asked deliberately, 'How's your mother?'

'She's all right,' Stan muttered.

'Good – then we'll get along, shall we? Can you drive?'

'No.'

'Pity. I'll have to teach you. A garage would be more

119

profitable than a cycle shop in this day and age.'

'I'm all right as I am, thanks.'

Teddy shrugged again. Then he shifted the weeping child from his lap, slid into the driver's seat, tucked her under his arms, and steered the car carefully between the groups of gaping children. With a nonchalant ease that riled Stan, who was pushing his bike on the icy road, Teddy's shining blue automobile crawled slowly up the High Street, and turned the corner.

The firelight flickered on the window, and a face peered anxiously into the gathering dusk. Stan had pushed his bicycle through the back gate and Annie was already standing at the open door as the car slid to a halt. Her hands covered her mouth as she whispered, 'Oh, *no!*' Her eyes were black in her flushed face.

The tall man in the long fur coat kicked open the gate and strode down the path carrying the child. She could see him clearly now – the lean, bronzed face and vivid blue eyes. He was smiling at her discomfort – the same smile that Miss Price had once declared could charm a bird off a bough.

In the low doorway he bent his head to kiss her cheek. 'Hullo, Annie, old girl! You're looking very well.' His voice was teasing. He was enjoying this particular home-coming.

Annie stared, speechless with shock, and wondered if she were dreaming. She had often wondered if he might turn up again one day, as destitute as a tramp, knowing he would always find a welcome. He was too much a part of those early years to forget or discard; too deeply involved in her married life – and the father of her four sons. For that reason alone he would claim the right to come home if he wished, she had told herself repeatedly in the past.

Now he was here. But this elegant, fur-clad gentleman, with an automobile, was beyond the scope of her limited ex-

120

pectation. It *was* Teddy, but a Teddy from another world. So she stared speechless, then her eyes dropped to the child, still sobbing convulsively, and he put the child in her arms and stepped inside.

His glance travelled round the room, and the lamplight revealed his greying hair as he dropped his cap and coat on a chair. In the pin-stripe suit with the padded shoulders, wide lapels and stove-pipe trousers, he looked like a tailor's dummy in that homely, old-fashioned room. His tie was adorned with red dragons, his socks purple, his patent-leather shoes had pointed toes, and gold cuff-links fastened the cuffs of his silk shirt. Teddy was so obviously showing off, Annie could see the boy in this aging man, and the old feeling of maternal protectiveness would not have him ridiculed, though he was rather ridiculous!

'You haven't changed anything,' he said with satisfaction, smoothing his well-oiled head. Then she saw the heavy seal of the signet ring, flashing in the light on his long, slender hand. She had always admired Teddy's beautiful hands, from that first day in the scullery at Merton Hall, because her own hands were ugly, with their stubby fingers, roughened and stained by hard work, wrinkled with years of immersion in hot soda water.

She stood the child down, unbuttoned her coat, took off her tammy, scarf and mittens, talking soothingly in her gentle way, while Teddy spread himself on the sofa, watching her with amused indulgence. This was the same little woman going through exactly the same process with her grandchild as she had with her own boys. But what was she doing here, this child? Had she lost her mother? Where were his other sons – Dick, Tom and Gordon? These questions had to be asked, but there was no urgency, for he would stay for a couple of days, meet all the family, distribute all the expensive presents in the case he had left in the boot of the car, then make his way back to London.

121

The child's face was blotched with crying, her eyes red-rimmed, her nose swollen. She was a plain little thing, he thought, but rather appealing, and he liked small girls – big girls too, for that matter!

Annie wiped the child's face, gave her a warm hug, then sat her down on Teddy's knee. She sighed, laid her head on his shoulder, and closed her eyes.

Stan came into the room through the scullery door, glanced at the pair on the sofa, and spoke to his mother. 'Have you brewed the tea?'

'Yes.'

The atmosphere was tense with Stan's resentment, for he could not bear to see Lucy so comfortably installed on his father's knee. But Teddy was relaxed and unconcerned as ever with the likes and dislikes of his children. At one time he had been jealous of playing second fiddle to the boys, but that was before he had enjoyed the satisfaction of security and independence. With a chip on his shoulder from the Boys' Home, and bad luck dogging his footsteps for years, no wonder he was so restless and unreliable; Teddy excused his young, irresponsible self, as Annie had excused him. He could always depend on Annie.

A starched white cloth covered the table and tea was laid ready – thin bread and butter, a dish of home-made jam – it looked like his favourite strawberry! – and the fruit cake, sparsely sprinkled with currants and raisins, and, of course, the candied peel. He and the boys always picked it out, but Annie still considered the peel was necessary to flavour a fruit cake. Dear old Annie! She could be a bit stubborn over some things, he thought, but today his thoughts were kind, tolerant, indulgent. He had come into his own at last, and had acquired both the money and the means to please himself. So he could afford to be generous. No need to rob that little fund for a rainy day. He glanced at the tea-caddy on the mantelpiece, remembering the shillings and

122

sixpences he had pilfered in the old days. Before he left he would slip in a ten-pound note, not because he was suffering from a guilty conscience, but to give Annie a surprise. She was not expecting him to sit up at the table for tea. She hadn't forgotten that he liked his tea in comfort, on the sofa. They smiled at each other as he took the cup.

'She's dropped off to sleep. She's tired out, poor mite,' she whispered.

Now it was Stan's turn to feel jealous, and he ate his tea at the table in sulky silence. Then he pushed back his chair, glowered at his father, and demanded aggressively, 'Isn't it about time you explained how you happen to be here, when you were reported dead, years ago?'

Teddy and Annie exchanged a meaningful glance.

'So you told the boys I was dead?' Teddy's voice was calm, his manner complacent.

Annie nodded, and he shrugged and turned to face Stan. 'If your mother told you I was dead, she must have had a very good reason,' he told his son. 'Your mother always had a good reason for covering up the transgressions of a ne'er-do-well husband. From a misplaced sense of loyalty she has told a good many lies on my behalf – bless her!' He smiled at Annie's distress with comforting reassurance, and went on, 'Let me explain. You boys have always been her whole world. She wanted children, but she didn't want a husband. It's unfortunate for a woman who is wholly maternal to have to sleep with a man in order to produce her offspring.'

Now Annie's face had flushed with embarrassment, and Stan was equally embarrassed.

'Some women make good mothers. Some make good wives. In all my travels, I have yet to meet a woman intelligent enough to combine both wife and mother in equal measure. Now I'm not suggesting your mother neglected me as a husband, far from it. She was most dutiful and she was fond of me, in her way. She may still be fond of me?'

Annie was crying quietly, Stan looked puzzled.

Teddy went on, 'Whatever she told you and your brothers seemed right, *at the time* – right for you boys – understand? Her first thought was always to protect you boys from a father invariably in some kind of trouble. It's strange, isn't it, but I had no paternal feelings at all, and looking at you now, I still have none. But then the feeling is mutual, for you have no feeling for me either.'

Stan made no answer, and Teddy turned to Annie again.

'Was it that last letter from the ship that decided you, my dear?' he asked gently.

'Yes.' Annie's voice was choked with tears.

'What happened to me?'

'You had an accident.'

'And got myself killed?'

'Yes.'

'You did well, my dear. Full marks for ingenuity!'

'Don't!' she pleaded. 'I – I thought they were too young to understand about – about you getting married again, and somehow I never got around to telling them the truth.'

Teddy turned back to his silent son, and explained carefully, as to a child. 'I told your mother in the letter I was going to marry again – bigamously. It was the end of our marriage. I was never coming back. She did right to tell you I was dead. But it so happens we are still legally married, your mother and I.' He smiled at Annie's startled exclamation and added, soothingly, 'Don't worry, old girl. I'm not intending to claim my right to the marriage bed! It may surprise you to know I've lost my taste for love-making. Perhaps it serves me right for I asked for it, and I knew the type of woman she was before I lived with her. A steward's job on board ship is very enlightening, and it was a long voyage. We both knew what we wanted. As a wealthy widow she made no secret of the fact that her first husband

124

had disappointed her. She was looking for a second husband, preferably young, good-looking and virile – I answered to that description!' His blue eyes mocked his son's disgusted expression. 'I had no scruples, as your mother will testify. When I wanted something, I usually managed to get it, by fair means or foul. I wanted to get away from everything connected with the old life. I hated it! I wanted security *and* independence, but it was too much to expect both, I suppose. In a way I lost my independence with that woman. She was the boss, for she held the purse – the servants despised me. If I wasn't so fundamentally lazy, I would have left her, but that would have meant working for a living again.'

His weak mouth twisted with the memory, then he shrugged it away and went on with the story of those lost years.

They were listening intently now, and Teddy had always loved an audience. If he exaggerated the role he had played in that far distant African province, he could be forgiven for every story-teller is allowed a certain licence to use his imagination. Annie was gazing at him in silent admiration, for she had always known he would please himself, and make his way in the world. He was coming to the end of his story and the child on his knee had not stirred in the telling. Her head still rested comfortably on his padded shoulder.

'The past two years have been a bit of a strain,' he admitted. 'She was a sick woman and I helped to nurse her. When she died, she left everything to me, apart from several small legacies to the older servants. That was six months ago. I sold the place to our nearest neighbour, and made straight for London. There's no place like London if you've the means to enjoy it. I've taken one of those nice service flats near Regent's Park, only a short distance from the Zoo. Lucy must come and stay with me.'

He could see the relief on those two tense faces, and Stan

spoke abruptly. 'I've got a job to finish,' and slipped away.

Annie pushed back the chair and went to sit beside Teddy and the child on the sofa. And he flung his arm about her shoulders and laid his cheek against her cheek.

'Good old Annie. I knew I could depend on you to understand,' he said gratefully. They sat there in the firelight, while the child slept exhausted. They had never been so close or so near to that harmonious relationship between a man and a woman with so many differences to separate them.

'Stan still hates me.' Teddy was merely stating a fact, but it saddened Annie. 'Tell me about the others – Dick, Tom and Gordon. Are they doing well?' he asked.

It was the moment she had been expecting and dreading, yet it was typical of Teddy to want to tell his own story first. Now she sighed, and moved her head restlessly on his padded shoulder. It was strangely comforting, this padded shoulder, and his arm had tightened about her own shoulders. Her voice was scarcely audible as she told her sad saga of the lost years, and there was no other sound to disturb them but the distant hum of a treadle machine in the workshop.

She began by telling of Gordon's treachery, and the consequent death of Stan's Kathie in childbirth.

'Like father, like son,' Teddy murmured. 'My God! What I have to answer for!'

Then Annie went on to tell of Tom and his blindness.

'But that's terrible,' he said, and she could see he was deeply moved. 'When can I see him?' he asked, and she told him they always came to visit her on Sunday, in time for dinner, and stayed till after tea, so he would see his four other grandchildren and Tom's wife, Ruby, who was such a splendid little woman.

But Annie's voice was choked when she started to tell of Dick's accident in the hop-garden in September of last

126

year. Teddy squeezed her shoulders affectionately, his own eyes wet. What could he say to comfort her when she covered her face with her hands and wept? It was too late. She had borne the burden of these tragedies alone.

Teddy was shamed at last, and so eager to make amends he began forthwith to make wonderful plans for the future, even while Annie wept beside him. The cheque book in his pocket was still a novelty, and he visualised Annie going to the post office to bank the cheques. It did not occur to him that she would refuse to accept money, though Stan had so curtly refused the offer of a garage, to replace the cycle shop. For Teddy, money was the answer to any problem. Money could talk. Money could pave the path with ease, settle old scores, and pour oil on troubled waters. But neither his wife nor his son would want a share in these wonderful plans for their future, for they were content with their simple way of life.

Lucy was another matter, so Teddy's generosity would not be entirely rejected. Dick's child must not be denied the education he had intended for her.

Now Teddy remembered the big, bulging suitcase he had left in the car, and he sat the sleeping child on Annie's lap and hurried out to get it, with the eagerness of a boy awaiting appraisal for his thoughtfulness. His presents for the boys, as he remembered them, were most suitable, but, alas, they came too late for Dick, Tom and Gordon, and only brought the tears to Annie's eyes again when he spread them on the table for her inspection – a set of tools for Stan, in the best quality steel – a set of leather-bound volumes of Shakespeare's plays for Dick – skates for Tom – and a large box of paints and brushes for Gordon. It was disconcerting and disappointing to Teddy's well-meaning gesture, to have all but one of his handsome gifts replaced in the case, and Stan only accepting the tools reluctantly after his mother's pleading.

127

The fur cape, for which he had paid a princely sum at Harrods, draped her plump shoulders most becomingly. She was still so ridiculously like Mrs Noah, and the beautiful cape was obviously intended for a tall, elegant lady in an evening gown. What matter if it pleased her to have such a gift, and pleased Teddy to bestow it. It would, no doubt, be carefully packed away in tissue paper and mothballs, together with the other expensive presents Teddy had brought home from foreign parts in his younger days.

As for the grandchildren, he had not even contemplated, they must all have presents to celebrate his homecoming.

'I shall go to Tunbridge Wells tomorrow,' he told Annie, with renewed excitement in the pleasing of the new generation. 'You must advise me, my dear, on what to buy for Tom's children, and Lucy will tell me what she would like.'

When she awoke at last he fed her with scrambled egg and strips of buttered toast, coaxing her to eat. And she looked up at him with her grave, trusting eyes, that were so like Annie's. Already there seemed to be an affinity between them that surprised Annie and irritated Stan.

'This is your grandfather, dear,' Annie explained gently, but Teddy had instantly reminded her that he didn't *look* like a grandfather, and certainly did not feel like one!

'You can call me Uncle Ted,' he told the child.

But Tom's two little girls regarded him as a kind of fairy godfather when they discovered the presents that awaited them the following Sunday – a handsome doll's pram for Rosie and a scooter for Maudie. As for Sammy, he would spend many happy hours riding the rocking-horse and Charlie would dash up and down the cinder path in his new pedal car.

Lucy had to be urged to *think hard*, for she was not yet fully recovered from the shock of hearing that compelling order from an utter stranger: 'STAND STILL! – YOU

128

LITTLE FOOL! – STAND STILL!'

'I don't want anything, thank you,' she answered, politely, and shook her head when Teddy insisted that a little girl of seven must want something.

'I only want my Daddy,' she told him, gravely. And he scooped her up and hugged her with more warmth than he had ever shown towards his own boys when they were young.

'I'll take her with me in the car to Tunbridge Wells and she can choose her own present,' he told Annie.

'But she has to go to school,' Annie protested. 'We shall be in trouble with the Attendance Officer again.'

'Leave him to me. I'll deal with the tiresome fellow!' Teddy promised, and was amply rewarded by Lucy's shy smile of approval.

'How would you like to go to school with kind nuns to teach you and no rough children to bully you?' he asked, indulgently.

And Annie protested again. '*Not* the convent – but they're *Catholics!*'

'Don't worry, my dear, they won't make a little Catholic of Lucy without your sanction, and a convent education is universally recognised as the best for girls.'

'But you must give me time to think about it. I'm not used to making up my mind so suddenly on such important matters,' Annie insisted, with some dignity.

'Take your time, old girl. I don't want to hustle you.' Teddy's blue eyes held the old mockery, and she knew he would have his way about this new issue as he had in the past.

With Lucy's arms about his neck and the comforting reassurance of the child's recovery, Annie's little world was due for a change, whether she liked it or not. This prosperous gent from another world was still the head of the family.

129

Teddy winced involuntarily at the hard grip of Tom's calloused hand that Sunday morning, as Annie stood watching anxiously in the doorway. There was no response, no smile of welcome on his son's face. Like his brother Stan, Tom had no feeling for this man and was too honest to pretend.

'Hullo, Dad, so you've turned up again, eh – like the bad penny!' he added maliciously.

'Tom!' Ruby protested, giving him a playful push to mind his manners. She was obviously impressed by her father-in-law's appearance, and considered he had beautiful taste in clothes. They smiled at each other approvingly, and Teddy kissed her mouth that smelled strongly of aniseed balls. The whole family had been sucking aniseed balls on the two mile walk from the farm on the icy roads, this bleak day of January. Charlie was riding on Tom's broad back, and Sammy in the old push-chair with the carpet seat and the wobbly wheels. He waved his arms excitedly when he saw the big, shining automobile, and Teddy lifted him carefully into the driver's seat, and knew a moment of intense satisfaction in the joy and surprise on that small, peaked face. Then he kissed the two little girls, removed Charlie from Tom's back, and sent them indoors to find their presents. Their squeals of excitement, and Ruby's grateful hug for her own present – a fur tippet that he draped over her shabby tweed coat, did much to dispel the disapproval on Tom's sullen face.

That plucky little woman has a difficult time with that son of mine, he was thinking. But here's one person who won't refuse my cheque. Tom mustn't know.

'I didn't know what to get you, Tom. Then your mother suggested you might like a proper harness for the dog. This is leather, and it has a solid handle you can grip more easily. What do you think?' Teddy's self-confidence and self-importance crumbled in the company of Tom. He was a

130

little afraid of this sturdy man with the uplifted, listening face and bright eyes that seemed to be staring at him directly.

It was Ruby who exclaimed about the beautiful quality of the new harness, then went down on her hands and knees to unfasten the old, and fasten the new, on the quiet, patient dog. She put the handle into Tom's reluctant hand and bade him take a little walk with the dog to try it out. But he stood there, scowling like a bad-tempered boy, and she shook her head and shrugged her thin shoulders in a gesture of defeat that Teddy found pathetically eloquent of her life with her young blinded husband.

'Thanks,' said Tom, gruffly, and Ruby turned her attention to her four excited children, and her face brightened again.

'It's ever so good of you, Uncle Ted, to spend all this money on the kids. They ain't never seen such toys an' not loikly to on our bloody wages!' She laughed her shrill Cockney laugh, and Tom's face flinched.

'Poor devil. She's doing it on purpose,' Teddy thought.

Then Maudie piped up, like an echo of her mother. 'What you got, Lucy?'

'Nothing,' said her cousin. 'I didn't want anything.'

'Nuffink?' screeched Maudie, ringing the bell of her new scooter. 'Gahn! You're kidding!'

'Maudie!' Tom's voice was stern.

'Yes, Dad?'

'Stop showing off. Speak properly.'

'Yes, Dad.'

Ruby led the way into the garden, with the dog in his new harness, followed by Rosie with the handsome doll's pram in which two of Lucy's dolls were riding – Maudie hopping experimentally on the scooter – Charlie hooting and yelling in his pedal car. The garden path was slippery with ice and they skidded and shrieked as they made their way towards

131

the boundary hedge. Sammy was riding the rocking-horse, his puny legs encased in calipers, the empty stirrups rattling as he swung back and forth.

'Where are you, Mum?' Tom's voice was peevish.

'I'm here, Tom. Come and see the white mice. They've grown quite a bit since last Sunday.' She took his hand and squeezed it reassuringly. 'It's too cold for them outside now. They must stay in the scullery till the weather changes. On top of the copper is quite a good place for them, but I have to remove them on washing day!' she chuckled, as she opened the cage and took out a tiny furry creature with pink eyes. Tom's clenched fist opened to receive it and his clouded face instantly brightened. She knew how to please him, for he had a way with animals, big and small, this son of hers. Once upon a time, Stan was kept busy building cages and hutches to house the rabbits, guinea pigs and white mice at the bottom of the garden. It was Tom who always had a dog for company when he went exploring in the woods and fields, and Tom who fed the birds in winter when he was only a little lad. Yet Tom had been the most daring and the noisiest of her four boys.

She stood there, watching, while the savoury smells of roasting meat and potatoes drifted out to the scullery. Lucy was helping Stan to lay the table. Teddy had draped himself on the sofa, feeling the satisfaction of a benevolent uncle.

Tom's fingers stroked the quivering little creature in the palm of his hand till it lay quiet, its tiny heart throbbing. When Ruby burst in with the dog, he gave the mouse to Annie and she put it back in the cage. The dog clawed at his legs, and he bent to pat its head and run his hand along the new harness. 'Not bad, eh?' was all he said, but Annie and Ruby both knew the bad mood had passed.

Lucy was arranging the four tablespoons when her noisy cousins swarmed back into the room. She looked at them gravely and announced, in her cool, precise voice, 'I've thought of something I would like from Uncle Ted. I would like a small little locket to hang round my neck – and a picture of my Daddy inside.'

They stared at her in silence, then Teddy opened his arms and she slipped into them, smiling, stroking his face.

It was odd, Ruby was thinking, that Dick's child always seemed to steal the limelight from her own children. There was something rather special about Lucy.

So began a new chapter for the family – an exciting chapter for Annie's grandchildren, who never knew when Uncle Ted would suggest an outing in the fabulous automobile, or spend a couple of days with Annie, spoiling everyone with such boyish exuberance even Stan was weaned away from his distrust of the man who answered to the name of Uncle Ted.

'You see, Stan,' Annie explained carefully to her suspicious firstborn, 'your father had a chip on his shoulder for years, because he was labelled an orphan from the Boys' Home. It didn't worry me that I was never told about my parents, or how I came to be there in the Girls' Home. But it worried your father. Even as a young lad when I first met him at Merton Hall, he was fretting to get away from the working class. He was so sure that he had a right to a place in a better class of society, and he would never accept his proper place. Mind you, he could have been right, for he always had the look of being well-bred. He still has. If only you and Tom would let bygones be bygones, and forget his faults. He's doing his best to make amends, now that he's come into money. Lucy loves him for his own sake, so there must be some good in him for children always know. Tom's children love him for the presents and the treats he provides. And Ruby dotes on him because he gives her money. You call that bribery, and Tom has to be kept in ignorance

133

of what Ruby actually receives, but she deserves every penny. They were so poor. She probably fritters away most of it, for she's a bad manager, but what can you expect the way she was brought up? To please me, Stan, will you try not to be so critical of your father?'

'All right, Mum. Have it your way. I won't say another word,' Stan agreed. 'But don't ask me to like him!' he added, meaningly.

*　　　*　　　*

The promised visit to the Zoo was postponed till Easter Monday, because the weather was bad, and the long hard winter seemed never ending that year. In the meantime, there was the outing to the pantomime in Tunbridge Wells to be enjoyed, followed by tea at the old-established tea-rooms in the Pantiles, where Lucy ate sparingly of dainty bread and butter and Madeira cake, and Tom's children stuffed themselves with buttered muffins, cream cakes and doughnuts, followed by strawberry ices. Ruby kept pace with the children, for it was obviously the first time in her life that she had seen such a bountiful spread, and been urged to eat till she couldn't swallow another crumb. She was still at heart the same Cockney child from the East End, and Teddy was amused not shamed by her frequent lapses into the old rough language of the streets.

Before they went off to the Zoo at Easter, however, a new Tansad was delivered to the farm cottage by Carter Paterson, and the little old push-chair with the carpet seat was put aside till Sammy started school. The new Tansad was big enough to take both boys, and it had a hood and a mackintosh cover for Sammy's legs – which was just as well, since it rained all day on Easter Monday!

They went off in high spirits, with Ruby in the front, nursing Charlie, Sammy wedged between Teddy and

134

Ruby, and the three girls in the back. All were dressed in summer clothes, for it was the custom in the country to put away winter clothes at Easter, with no regard to the weather. Teddy was wearing a light suit and a panama hat, and all the family arrived back looking sadly bedraggled, but still cheerful.

They had spent some time in the monkey house, the aquarium, and the house of tropical birds, but Ruby's children were fretting to ride the elephant, so they all took their place in the long queue. Ruby took the two girls on the big elephant, while Sammy and Charlie were hoisted on to the baby elephant. Lucy shook her head decidedly and clung to Teddy's hand.

'They were so smelly,' she told him, 'especially the camel – or was it a dromedary?' – but Ruby's children insisted on riding twice over the appointed route. Teddy and Lucy shared a large umbrella during this part of the outing. Then it was time for tea, and another good feed of cream cakes and ice-cream. With their straw hats drooping, and their wet straggling hair draping their shoulders, Rosie and Maudie were looking decidedly the worse for wear by teatime. Sammy's clean shirt was stained with orange drink, and Charlie's white sailor suit smeared with chocolate ice-cream. (Annie bought most of their clothes for a few shillings at the jumble sales in the village hall.) Ruby's children seemed to collect dirt and spilled food and drinks, no matter where they happened to be. Teddy was glad to shepherd his grubby little tribe into the car and start for home.

Only Lucy was still clean and neat. He could always depend on Lucy! He was proud of her, and she was proud of him. She thought he was wonderful. He made everyone happy. He made them laugh. He was terribly extravagant with everything, even with his hugs and kisses. It was nice to be cuddled by someone smelling of scented hair oil and

135

not carbolic soap! Next to Daddy, Uncle Ted was the nicest man in her little world, though she felt a little guilty in putting him before Uncle Stan and Uncle Tom, because he was so new. It pleased Granny enormously that they loved each other, for she wanted everyone to love Uncle Ted. There was never any question that he would want to share Granny's bed. That would have been awful! It was *her* place and *her* privilege, to curl up beside her dear, warm, comfortable Granny, though she was a big girl now.

There was something rather special about an uncle who could whisk you out of the village school and the clutches of the bullies from Baker's Row, straight into the arms of the sweet nuns of the Convent of the Holy Child.

Chapter Six

Ten years passed – years of inevitable change for Annie's grandchildren – but Teddy still enjoyed the best of both worlds, with his comfortable service flat near London's Regent's Park, and his family in the country he could visit whenever he felt inclineed. And, of course, he enjoyed playing host to the family, providing they gave him good notice and did not arrive en masse!

Even Annie had been persuaded to visit him for a week, after the hop-picking season that first year. It was her first holiday, and Teddy so kind and thoughtful she now regarded the regular break in her normal routine with happy anticipation.

Ruby left Tom in the care of the two girls for a week at Easter, and the boys went with her to London. At Whitsun it was the girls' turn to visit Uncle Ted.

Lucy was Teddy's favourite visitor, and he found it difficult to be impartial with his invitations, when he would have liked Lucy's company indefinitely during the school holidays. For Annie's sake, he had become quite conscientious of recent years, for she was the one to suffer from Ruby's sharp tongue if Tom's children were not treated fairly. And Stan must not be upset by Lucy's long absence, for he loved Dick's child as his own.

During the long summer holidays, when Annie joined Tom and Ruby and their children in the hop-garden every year, Lucy enjoyed several weeks of freedom with her two uncles – the quiet uncle who escorted her by bicycle to the quaint villages of the Weald of Kent, and the gay uncle, with his big expensive car, and lavish ideas for entertainment of his little favourite. They drove in style to Hampton Court and Kew Gardens, and lunched in the best restaurants – no picnic meals for Teddy!

When the weather was too wet for these excursions, they would wander round museums and art galleries. The evenings were usually spent at a concert or a cinema. Sometimes, when Lucy was tired after an exciting day, they would stay in, play duets on the piano, and listen to records. For Lucy's sake, Teddy had cultivated a taste for Chopin and Mozart. They played chess with an earnest concentration that would have surprised Annie. Teddy even learned to speak a little elementary French in order to read the menu at the posh restaurant they frequented in Jermyn Street!

In Lucy's company he was careful to curb his language and his extravagant taste in men's fashion, for she liked to see him dressed like a gentleman, and her own tastes were simple as she grew into adolescence.

Teddy entertained Tom's two girls in Lyons' Corner House, fish and chip bars and noisy cafés, to the accompaniment of the latest dance hits. They loved the music hall and the street markets of Portobello Road and Whitechapel, and he bought the kind of cheap trinkets he had once bought for Muriel, in those far off days as a postman, in that quiet village. While Lucy would enjoy cooking their supper and brewing coffee in his modern kitchen, her cousins would bring back their supper of fish and chips, washed down with strong tea.

Lucy had accepted the luxury of fitted carpets, a bathroom with a constant flow of boiling hot water, and a lavatory with a flush, quite naturally, and never made the mistake of comparing Uncle Ted's London flat with Granny's old-fashioned country cottage, when she returned home. The two worlds were set far apart, and she

138

knew where she rightly belonged.

Tom's girls came back to their cramped farm cottage with glowing tales of the luxury they had enjoyed, and made his life miserable for days in comparing the two establishments. But it did not affect the boys that way, for they were essentially Tom's children, country born and bred.

With a fond Granny, two doting uncles, and a bosom friend called Mary Smith, together with the sweet nuns at the Convent – though Sister Theresa and Sister Evangeline could be stern if you misbehaved! – Lucy enjoyed a happy childhood, with only brief moments of sadness, wishing her gentle, intelligent father had lived to share it.

Mary Smith was a nice ordinary child, with no special talents, but a sweet nature that Lucy found endearing. Her parents were missionaries in China, which may have accounted for it. Since the two girls could not bear to be parted for the long school vacations – Lucy was a weekly boarder – Mary would spend part of the holiday at Annie's cottage and Teddy's flat, wherever Lucy happened to be, and she always spent Christmas with Annie's family. Both girls had decided at the age of twelve to choose nursing as a career when they left school at seventeen.

'Why nursing? It's such a hard life, and you are not very strong,' Teddy argued, but they were determined.

'My mother was a nurse, and I *do* remember her,' she reminded him, wistfully.

It was the first time Lucy had mentioned a mother she had not seen since the age of four. Lucy was a serious minded girl, bent on a dedicated vocation, and in this she had Annie's full approval.

As for Tom's girls – Rosie married the cowman's eldest boy at sixteen, with her first baby born seven months later!

'What's all this?' Tom demanded, truculently, when told he was already a grandfather.

'Premature,' Ruby explained, with bland innocence.

It was not the first time one of Tom's children had deceived him. 'Don't tell your Dad,' had saved a lot of trouble in the past, and would do so again, for Ruby knew how to manage him.

Maudie had ambitions, and no intention of spending the rest of her life in a farm cottage with damp walls and an earth closet. Only one person could gratify such ambition, and he was willing to pay her fees at the Secretarial Training College in Tunbridge Wells, and her board and lodging at a hostel in the town. Maudie never went back to live in that cramped little cottage; she returned only for short visits, to please her mother. She made straight for London, and the luxury of her own bed-sitting-room in Bayswater – and a job in a typing pool of a big insurance company in the City.

Sammy and Charlie would be needed on the farm when another war robbed the farmer, for the second time, of his young labourers.

Stan had obligingly moved out of the bedroom when Lucy brought Mary home. From the age of eight Mary was part of the family, and Annie was 'Granny'. It was strange to have the big marriage bed to herself again after so many years with a small child tucked in beside her; strange to hear the two young girls talking and giggling in the adjoining room, to see their clothes hanging in the wardrobe, and the drawers full of the clutter that girls collect.

Stan had moved into the hut in the garden, originally built as a workshop for Tom when he came home blinded after the war. With a camp bed, chest of drawers, a chair, a couple of shelves, a strip of matting and a row of hooks behind the door, the hut was furnished according to Stan's simple requirements. He still had the Scout troop to occupy all his spare time, and was glad of this absorbing interest when Lucy attached herself to Mary. As the older boys left to start work, younger brothers stepped into their shoes, and often into their uniforms, for many of the boys came from large families and poor homes. Two by two they would take their turn to sit on the sagging old sofa before a blazing fire on a winter evening, to pass a test for a particular badge. Cocoa was the favourite beverage on those winter evenings, and from Easter till the end of hop-picking season, the big crock on the larder floor was never empty of lemonade. Several of the boys who lived in the hamlet some three miles from the village, would come in after school on Tuesday, have a good tea, and wait to join the rest in the Scout hut at six o'clock.

Annie enjoyed having the boys about the place. She was lost without children. They would borrow her big flat irons and damp cloths to press the brims of their hats, and her Brasso to polish buckles and badges. She often repaired a tear or mended a hole in a sock that some busy mother had overlooked.

On summer evenings, boys would be perched on the fence like a line of homing swallows, whittling whistles from hollow reeds, with their sharp penknives.

Sometimes Annie would borrow Rosie's baby for a few days, for the sheer joy of smelling that special smell of baby about the house. Napkins would be draped over the old brass fireguard again, and a drawer would serve as a cradle on the hearthrug. If Teddy's visit happened to coincide with the baby's, he would push the napkins aside and complain that he couldn't see the fire. It brought back memories of the young Teddy, so reluctant to accept the role of parenthood; so jealous of the time and attention the babies demanded of Annie. There was no need for jealousy now. Grandchildren could be enjoyed as they grew into adolescence. Each individual child had something to offer Teddy in its natural development. Ugly ducklings grew into lovely swans – like Maudie. Handicapped Sammy had an

141

amazing knowledge of the wild creatures and their habitats, within the radius of the few miles he could cover on his crippled legs. It pleased Teddy almost as much as the boy to buy the illustrated books on nature study he had long coveted in the fascinating bookshop in Charing Cross Road. Sammy had grown into a quiet contented lad, too shy to ask favours of a wealthy uncle with a fat purse. He still wore a caliper on one puny leg and limped badly.

'It don't worry me. You get used to it,' he invariably answered when a stranger sympathised with his handicap.

Teddy was not disposed to nurse an infant that christened him with the alarming title of great-grandfather. It was too much to expect of a dedicated Peter Pan! Besides, he couldn't risk the wetting of an expensive suit. When Annie offered him the baby, clean and sweet-smelling after its bath, Teddy would shiver apprehensively and ward it off with both hands.

'You haven't changed. You never would nurse your own babies,' Annie chided him, but there were no tears of disappointment now, no malice in her chiding. Others changed, but not Teddy.

They had been expecting it for some time, since the fall of France, but when the letter came it had a London postmark. Annie opened it with trembling fingers, her cheeks flushed. She recognised Gordon's sprawling childish hand-writing on the envelope, because she had received a card from him every year at Christmas since he went away. She had never known his address in Paris, or whether he had prospered as an artist in his adopted country.

She had not expected to receive letters from Gordon. Tom and Stan had kept her posted during the First World War, with an occasional field postcard specially printed for the troops in Flanders. She had kept every one, as she had kept the ornate Christmas cards from Paris.

142

Now she read the letter aloud to Stan, and they stared at each other speechless for a long moment. It was brief, but it told them all they wanted to know.

Dear Mum,
I expect you have been a bit worried about me lately. Well, here we are. Safe and sound in London, all three of us. I married Marie-Lou when we knew we should have to leave France. She's quite a bit older than me, but we get along fine. She only speaks a few words of English, but I'm pretty good on the French lingo. Little Suzette is nearly six months old. We call her Susie. She looks like me. We are staying in a hostel with a lot of other refugees. We all had to leave in a hurry and only allowed to bring one small bag. It's very crowded and uncomfortable here, and Marie-Lou has asked me to write and see if you will have us for a few weeks, till we can find lodgings. She sends her love.
                    Your loving son,
                    Gordon.
P.S. We would like to live in London because we shall miss Paris.

'What shall we do, Stan?' Annie asked quietly. She could not have them here to upset Stan. Gordon had not troubled about her all these years, but for that one card at Christmas. Now he was in trouble and turned to her. It was natural that he should, and he had every right to come home when it suited him.

'We must have them here, of course. We shall manage. We always have managed, haven't we, Mum?' Stan was saying.

She sighed with relief. What would she do without Stan?

'The girls must give up their room for a while. They don't use it a lot these days, while they are doing their training at Tunbridge Wells Hospital. Anyway, they can come

143

home on their free days still, by bus. It's not far. We've got to remember, Mum, they can be sent anywhere in the country, possibly overseas, once they have finished their training. If it's going to be a long war, like the last one, we all have to face up to changes, whether we like it or not. Besides, we couldn't keep the room standing empty with Gordon and his family in need. No, they must come here.'

It was a long speech for Stan, who was not normally so articulate.

Annie agreed. 'But I still can't grasp it, Stan. Gordon married, with a child.'

'That Marie-Lou has probably been waiting for some time to get a wedding ring on her finger!' Stan commented dryly.

'My young brother was a past master at sliding out of responsibility, as we both know to our cost. It's my guess they have been living together for some time, and, but for the war, would still be living in sin, as they say. This Marie-Lou had the right idea, to tie him down with a child, for it's not so easy to escape the responsibility of fatherhood in another country. I imagine Gordon is still a British citizen. What does it matter, Mum? It's their life and they must live it any way they choose. We're old-fashioned, you and me!' He squeezed her shoulders affectionately, and she was grateful for his advice on yet another family problem.

'What a silly name, anyway. Short for Louise, I suppose? Why not Marie or Louise in that case?'

'She's French,' said Annie, sensibly, as though that excused any idiosyncracies in her new foreign daughter-in-law.

So Gordon and his little family arrived, and were made welcome. Even Gordon seemed alien, with his strange speech and behaviour. Annie had to keep reminding herself he was one of her boys, her own flesh and blood.

Not so Marie-Lou. They could never be reconciled in a

144

lifetime! She was a bossy, temperamental little woman, and obviously had Gordon under her thumb now that she had his ring on her finger. Everything she said was accompanied by excited gesticulations and shrugged shoulders, so that even the most unimportant matter appeared of vital importance. 'Darling' was the word she used most frequently. They all were her 'darlings', including the butcher and the grocer, from whom she soon wheedled extra provisions. It was a word as unfamiliar in Annie's small world as in the home of any working-class family. How could it mean a loving endearment when it was used so carelessly? Annie asked herself.

'I no like,' was constantly on the painted lips of Marie-Lou. The weather, the food, the quiet countryside, and the parcels of clothing she received from the hard-working ladies of the WVS, all were shrugged away with eloquent – 'I no like!' Husband and wife quarrelled a lot, for the sensual pleasure of reconciliation in bed.

It all surprised and distressed Annie, who was no match for this garrulous little woman her son had married. Stan kept out of their way. He was only obliged to meet them at mealtimes, for they were not interested in his workshop and could not understand his quiet contentment.

The baby was the one saving grace in these disturbing weeks, when nothing was normal, but Annie was not allowed to interfere in any way. The baby had a sour smell for she was left lying in wet napkins. Her little buttocks were red and sore, and she was sick after every hurried bottle, for Marie-Lou was too impatient, and Annie too reluctant to suggest her own comfortable lap. How could any mother not enjoy these sweet interludes in her busy day? It was inconceivable to Annie, where first consideration had been the care and comfort of her babies, and all else of secondary importance. Her grandchildren had soon discovered that warm, comfortable lap, and to be left with

145

Granny for a few days was a treat to be remembered in later years.

But Susie was a happy baby, who seemed to thrive on her parents' casual treatment; for Gordon had his father's aversion to babies, and no love for this blue-eyed cherub with the cap of golden hair, so like himself at the same age.

There were several occasions, however, during the three months they were living with Annie, when Gordon and Marie-Lou went off to London for the day, to meet their friends in Soho, and endeavour to persuade someone to offer them accommodation. Many of the refugees from Paris were still obliged to stay at the hostel, but several families had moved to the spacious vaults of the YMCA off Tottenham Court Road, and commandeered a small area of floor space for themselves. Others were sleeping on the crowded platforms of the Underground, where the authorities provided tiers of bunks, and the WVS an all-night canteen. Either arrangement would have suited Marie-Lou, for she was bored and miserable in the cottage with her in-laws who could not speak a word of French.

During their absence, Annie would devote the whole day to the enjoyment of Susie. Clean and sweet-smelling, dressed in the baby clothes she still kept in the fireside cupboard for sentimental reasons, they sallied forth to the village in the afternoon – a proud Granny showing off the latest addition to the family, in the second-hand pram an obliging neighbour had provided.

For the third time Gordon and his wife came back tired and disagreeable, with a bottle of French burgundy as consolation for their disappointment. Then, at last, on the fourth trip to London, they came back jubilant and slightly intoxicated. Annie and Stan were hugged and kissed by the exuberant Marie-Lou, and Susie, her little cabbage, tasted wine for the first time in her young life.

Gordon and his wife had been promised a temporary

lodging with an acquaintance in Soho – the widow of an English private in the First World War. The rooms of the third floor flat were small, and crowded with heavy furniture, but they would have a splendid view over the rooftops and easy access to the street market. Unfortunately, their prospective landlady had only one room to offer, and a strong objection to babies.

'Would you mind if we left Susie with you, Mum, for a week or two?' Gordon asked persuasively. 'We shall find a place of our own more easily once we are living in London. Besides, she will be safer here with you,' he added artfully.

Mind? Annie could not hide her joy and satisfaction in such an arrangement, or her relief in having the house to herself again. It had been an interminable three months with the dictatorial Marie-Lou.

'But aren't you scared of the Blitz?' she asked.

With the Luftwaffe bombers taking their heavy toll of casualties night after night, it seemed like madness. Stan thought so too, and they both tried to persuade them to change their minds, in a half-hearted way. Soho was the Mecca now for these homeless Parisians, and they would sooner face the hazards of the Blitz than the boredom of life in a country village. Only one stray bomb had been dropped in a quiet field, killing a couple of cows, and the incident had been the main topic of conversation in all three pubs for days.

Marie-Lou departed in a flood of sentimental tears, calling down blessings from Heaven on her saintly mother-in-law. Gordon promised to send money for Susie's support as soon as he started work as a waiter in a hotel. There would be hotel work for Marie-Lou, also, and good money to be made in tips. The future was bright. They would not be beggars. They could hold up their heads again. The Blessed Mother of God and all the saints would see that Annie was amply rewarded for all her kindness.

147

Gordon translated this emotional outburst with some impatience, for he wanted to get away. It had been a mistake, coming home, and utterly boring to play interpreter for his wife and his own relations.

In all these weeks, no mention was made of Teddy, and Annie had written to warn him to keep away. She did not want him to get involved with Gordon and Marie-Lou, for they would not only scrounge money but expect to be invited to share the flat. So Annie and Stan were careful to avoid the subject of a father presumed dead by his youngest son, and Tom and his family were advised not to mention Teddy's generosity. So he was spared a reunion and the consequent upheaval in his pleasant way of life, and they kept in touch by telephone. It was, for Annie, a nerve-racking experience that first call from the public telephone kiosk in the village post-office, and she never conquered her fear of the strange instrument, and left Teddy to do most of the talking. Yet she hurried to the rendezvous every Wednesday evening as eagerly as a young girl awaiting a call from her lover.

So many changes had been accepted in the quiet village in the past few months, and once again they were caught up in a war that spared neither the rich nor the poor. Merton Hall lost the son and heir of a new generation, and saw the end of an era for the Middleton family. Young servants would scorn domestic service after the war and the freedom they had enjoyed. Many of the old servants, long since retired to the cottages on the estate, had not lived to see the end of an era they had supposed would last for ever. Miss Price joined her sister in Torquay, so the last contact with Merton Hall was lost. It was a sad day for Annie when she said goodbye to such a loyal friend. Yet all around her mothers were losing sons and daughters to the war machine that was already swallowing up young lives on active service, as well as civilians on the home front. The boys

148

who were sitting on her sofa, drinking cocoa, only a couple of years ago, were parading proudly in new uniforms, coming to kiss her, and to shake hands with Stan. How many would be spared this time, they wondered. And would Freddy, Victor or bright-eyed Wally Pearce suffer the same unhappy fate as their Tom?

Strict rationing was enforced at the butcher's and grocer's, but the working-class in the country were still better off than their town counterparts, with fresh vegetables from their gardens and allotments, fresh fruit in season, and eggs from the few hens they managed to feed. Women like Annie Parsons had always fed their families. The Kaiser had not defeated them, and neither would Hitler.

But for Annie, her biggest worry was over as she waved farewell to Gordon and Marie-Lou, for they had not cared for her plain fare, her stews or her suet dumplings! Her small savings had been spent on bottles of wine they drank like water at every meal. Stan had increased her housekeeping allowance, but still it was not enough to satisfy their extravagant tastes. This was a thorn in the flesh to Annie and Stan, who had tried so hard to please them.

Standing at the gate with Stan and the baby, one Sunday morning, Annie lifted Susie's dimpled hand to wave as her parents climbed into the station taxi. The relief in their departure was tempered with sadness, since all four adults had been forced to admit it had been a mistake. The years had not erased the memory of that early tragedy, and Stan had been constantly reminded of his young wife during the time his brother lived under the same roof. It was no use, the bitterness was still there, though Kathie's name was never mentioned. On that same sofa, where Gordon cuddled Marie-Lou, he had seduced Stan's innocent child-wife.

No wonder he sighed with relief as the taxi pulled away.

149

'Let's have a cup of tea, eh, Mum?' he asked, as he followed her down the garden path. She nodded, too choked to speak, and when he had brewed the tea he handed her a cup and reminded her kindly, 'You did your best, Mum. I'm glad to see the back of them – and you've still got the baby,' he added, smiling at the child. 'I ought to see about making her a cot, for she's outgrown that drawer.'

'Susie will be sleeping with me, now,' Annie told him, quietly, as she cuddled the baby on her lap.

When the telegram was delivered, some six weeks later, informing Annie that her son and his wife had been killed in a raid, Annie was bathing the baby in a tin tub, on the hearth-rug. The firelight played on the old oak beams, and the patchwork shawl draped on the back of Stan's arm-chair.

Stan was surprised that she received the news so calmly. 'I've been expecting it. I had a premonition when they left we shouldn't see them again,' she told him.

They looked at the child with a single thought. 'She's safe here with us.'

Then Annie took up the tablet of Pears Soap, lathered the square of soft flannel, and sponged the child's firm, little body.